Go Big
or
Go Home

Books by Will Hobbs

Go Big or Go Home

WILL HOBBS

SCHOLASTIC INC.
New York Toronto London Auckland Sydney
Mexico City New Delhi Hong Kong Buenos Aires

ISBN-13: 978-0-545-15369-0
ISBN-10: 0-545-15369-7

12 11 10 9 8 7 6 5 4 3 2 1   9 10 11 12 13 14/0

Printed in the U.S.A.   40

First Scholastic printing, January 2009

Typography by Larissa Lawrynenko

this one's for Clay

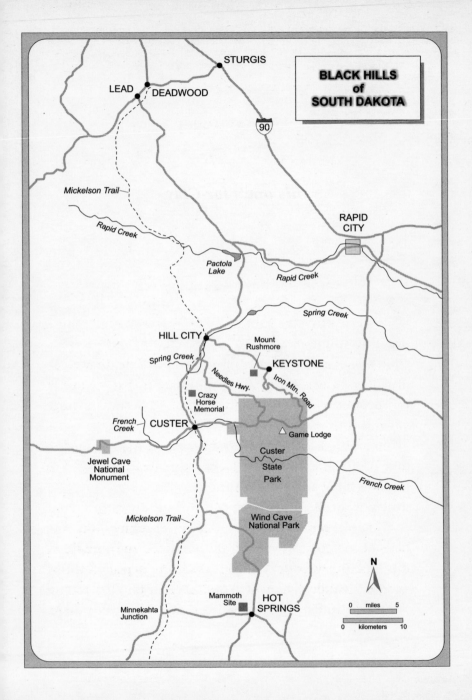

STURGIS

LEAD DEADWOOD

I-90

BLACK HILLS
of
SOUTH DAKOTA

Mickelson Trail

RAPID
CITY

Rapid Creek

Pactola
Lake

Rapid Creek

Spring Creek

HILL CITY

Mount
Rushmore

KEYSTONE

Spring Creek

Needles Hwy.

Iron Mtn. Road

Crazy
Horse
Memorial

French
Creek

CUSTER

Game Lodge

Custer
State
Park

French Creek

Jewel Cave
National
Monument

Mickelson Trail

Wind Cave
National Park

Mammoth
Site

HOT
SPRINGS

Minnekahta
Junction

N

0   miles   5

0   kilometers   10

The Intruder

THERE MIGHT BE MORE unlikely ways to die, but I can't think of any.

It was late in the evening at the end of the first week of August. I was home alone and sitting on the edge of my bed, only seconds from crashing. I let out a huge yawn.

In a way, I owe my life to my watch. As I reached to take it off, I had the vague feeling that I was supposed to do something at a certain time.

Do what, Brady?

Then I remembered. I'd been checking out the Perseid meteor shower off and on since the middle of July, and this was the night it was going to peak. I threw open my window, swiveled outside onto the flat roof of our garage, and pulled up the lawn chair I keep out there.

The sky was inky black and blazing with stars, which is nothing unusual for the Black Hills of South Dakota. Most nights are cloud-free, and our dry mountain air makes for excellent stargazing. Living out of town helps, too—no lights.

I'd barely found where to look—in front of the Perseus constellation—when the first shooting star fell, then another, and another.

What a show. I could read my watch by starlight alone, and I started timing them. Five to seven a minute!

Mars was hovering just above the treetops, brighter than any star and twinkling bloody red. Mars hadn't passed this close to Earth in a couple hundred years.

Too bad Quinn is missing the show, I thought. My cousin lived forty miles north in the town of Lead, which rhymes with *speed*. On Quinn's block the streetlights make for lousy stargazing.

I'd been outside awhile, long enough to feel the chill, and was about to crawl back inside and hit the sack. My dad might be getting home soon, but he wasn't expecting me to wait up.

All was quiet except the burbling of Spring Creek and a slight breeze in the pines. Nothing unusual was happening. Then, in a split second, something *totally* unusual was happening: the sky was changing from black to blue.

Horizon to horizon, the night sky was glowing a brilliant blue. My jaw was on the ground. Strange, beautiful, bizarre, eerie, weird, awesome . . . words can't begin to describe that light.

Then, suddenly, *BOOM! BOOM!* Two tremendous explosions rocked the sky, so powerful they rattled my bedroom window. What in the world?

I didn't know what to make of the blue light, but I wondered if the booms had come from the Crazy Horse Memorial five miles south, where they're carving a mountain into the biggest statue in the world. Lately my dad and his crew had been widening the gap between Crazy Horse's pointing arm and the mane of his warhorse. Saturday evenings in the summer, like this one, they do a night blast for the tourists. It's totally spectacular. From home we sometimes hear a muffled rumble, but nothing like this.

I didn't have time for another thought. All at once, a roar and a blinding fireball were coming down on me like a freight train strapped to a runaway skyrocket. I hit the deck, and as I did, *WHAM!* Something crashed right into the house. From the earsplitting sound of it, I'd nearly got hit.

Blinking and stupefied, I got to my feet, amazed to discover I was among the living. The sky was black again and lit with stars. Except for the burbling creek, everything was dead quiet.

Meteorite? I wondered. Could that be possible?

I climbed back through the window into my bedroom. When I switched on the light, more strangeness awaited. My bed was littered with debris—bits of wood, chunks of plasterboard, shreds of asphalt shingle. My eyes went to the ceiling over my bed and found

3

a ragged hole there, big as a softball.

I glanced back to my bed. The sheet was ripped open and scorched, right where I would have been lying. I stuck my fist into the hole and pushed it all the way through my foam mattress. Whatever had done this had punched a hole between two of the slats spanning my bed frame. I couldn't reach any farther, so I dropped to my knees and looked under the bed. And there it was, among splinters on the floor, unbelievably real. A meteorite!

Heart hammering, I sat on the edge of my bed with my prize in one palm and then the other. The space rock looked like a baked potato, all burned shiny, but with rougher edges, pits, and sparkles. It was heavy, and almost too hot to handle, as well it might be after blazing a fiery hole through the atmosphere. We'd been hit by an intruder from outer space! I couldn't think of anything cooler that had happened in my entire life.

I grabbed my cell and punched in Quinn's number.

Quinn on the Line

I KEPT HITTING THE REDIAL. Finally, Quinn. The TV was turned up loud. "What's up, Brady?" my cousin hollered.

"I just took a shower—know what kind?"

"What kind?"

"Meteor shower."

"Just heard about it. They're saying the sky turned blue."

"Like you wouldn't believe. I saw the whole thing!"

"Lucky stiff. The TV station in Rapid City said it could be seen from all over the Black Hills, even in other states. They said they'd just talked to an expert from the museum in Hill City."

"What'd he say?"

"From the brightness, the meteorite had some size to

it. After it exploded, a few chunks might've made it all the way to the ground without burning up, but probably they won't ever be found."

"He was wrong about that."

"What are you talking about, Brady?"

"I'm holding one in my hand right now."

"You lie like a rug."

"It came through the roof."

"Your roof? What does it look like?"

"Green asphalt shingles, brown trim . . ."

"The *meteorite*, you fungus. Tell me about the meteorite."

"What can I say? It crashed through the roof and went clear through my bed."

"Lucky you weren't in the sack. You would've been dead."

"Tell me about it."

I knew what Quinn was going to say next. He was going to deploy one of his two favorite words, *extreme* and *insane*, maybe both.

"Brady," he said. "That's extreme. That's insane!"

"I know, it's extremely insane."

"Dude, fate had you in its crosshairs. You dodged a space bullet."

"So, when are you coming down here to check it out?"

"Tomorrow."

"That quick? What about your job at the restaurant?"

"I just quit."

"Can you get your dad to bring you down here?"

"No problem."

I hung up grinning. It never takes Quinn long to make up his mind. Like when he's playing basketball, for example. He can slash to the hoop or stop on a dime and go vertical with that smooth, deadly jumper of his. You can't tell from his eyes. He's not even thinking about it. It's all instinct.

Still, Quinn doesn't always score. How was he going to talk his dad into this? They'd been going through a rough patch ever since Uncle Jake lost his job back in May.

One thing was for sure. Quinn had to get here. My summer had been a bust without him. He'd always come down to our place outside of Hill City for a couple of weeks every summer, sometimes even a month. The stuff we'd get into, our parents had no idea.

I heard my dad's pickup pull in. A minute later, his footsteps were on the porch. Once inside, he called softly from the foot of the stairs.

"I'm still up," I called back, then went to the landing where he could look up and see me. My dad was wearing his dusty overalls. He's a big guy, and solid as granite.

All serious, I said, "Dad, we've had a break-in."

"Really? Where?"

"My bedroom."

His face fell. "I hope you weren't home."

"I'm afraid I was."

"You scared him off?"

"Found him hiding under the bed."

By now I wasn't doing such a great job keeping a straight face. My dad looked mighty relieved. "Raccoon? Squirrel?"

"Space traveler," I replied. I brought the intruder from behind my back, then spilled my story as my dad came upstairs and checked out the damage. He'd seen the fireball from Crazy Horse, heard the big booms. "Pretty amazing," he concluded with a bearlike yawn. "Glad you're alive, son. We'll patch the roof in the morning."

It was disappointing to have my dad's exhaustion trump his amazement, but it had been an especially long day on the mountain. He headed down the hall for a quick shower and then to bed.

It would take awhile for me to settle down. I was as wired as if I'd knocked off Grabba Java in Hill City and drank all their coffee. I tiptoed downstairs and played a couple of video games I'd gotten from Quinn, *Skateboarding for the Insane* and *Snowboarding for the Insane.*

It was around 1:00 when I cleared the mess off my bed, stuffed some old T-shirts into the hole in my mattress, and hit the sack, meteorite in hand. I tossed and turned, ending up on my side with the space rock pressed against my chin, shot-put style. I could picture it slinging around and around the sun as a meteoroid for millions and millions of years. I could imagine its view of the rings of Saturn, the moons of Jupiter, the giant volcano on Mars, and our own phenomenal blue planet.

What must it have been like, your fireball ride down to Earth? Were you afraid you were going to fall into oblivion on the bottom of the ocean? Welcome to the Black Hills, space traveler. By the way, they're just *called* hills. Actually they're mountains, and black is how their forests make them look from way out on the prairie.

It seems I neglected to set the traveler on my nightstand before drifting off. I slept as soundly as the meteorite and woke up with it against the corner of my mouth and covered with drool.

Nice, Brady. Remember not to tell Quinn about this if he shows up.

He better show up.

I fretted over breakfast. "Maybe I should call up to Lead. Find out what's going on with Quinn and Uncle Jake."

Like I knew he would, my dad took a long sip of coffee. He was working up to saying, "Let's wait and see."

He took another long sip. "Let's wait and see," he said finally. "Let's let them work this out between the two of them."

My dad hates to talk on the telephone, and the same goes for his brother. Either one would just as soon pick up a poisonous snake.

Uncle Jake had been laid off from the Homestake Mine at the end of May. As far as we knew, he still hadn't found another job. My mom had nudged my dad into calling his brother every couple of weeks during June and July. The last I'd heard, Uncle Jake was still "exploring his options."

One thing was for sure, his job with Homestake wasn't coming back. After a century and a quarter, the richest gold mine in the history of the United States had finally ground to a halt. It had been sputtering the last ten years.

The way I understood it, families were managing to stay in Lead if they had two incomes. A lot of the mothers were working in Deadwood, just a couple of miles away. Deadwood had a slew of hotels and restaurants, and thirty-some casinos. The fathers, in search of a bigger paycheck, worked far away and drove huge distances to get home to their families as many weekends as they could.

With only one income, how was Quinn's dad going to manage to keep their home in Lead? Quinn's mother had died before he could even remember her, back when he was only three. From then on it had been just Quinn and his dad.

"So, what do you think Uncle Jake's going to come up with?" I asked as I was clearing the dishes. "What kind of options has he been exploring?"

"Last time we talked, he mentioned Wyoming. The gas fields are booming over there. He said he might have to go over there and check it out."

"Has he?"

"Not that I know of. But he'll have to soon, with school starting in three weeks."

"Quinn would go with him, move to Wyoming?"

My dad raised his huge hand. "Whoa," he said. "I have no idea what's going to happen."

"Maybe Quinn could live with us."

"I don't suppose that's outside the realm of possibility. One thing I know for sure, we have to let them figure this out for themselves, no interference from us. Uncle Jake wouldn't have it any other way. I want you to respect that, Brady. My guess is, your call last night got some serious discussion going, which is why we haven't heard from them."

"Reality bites," I said.

"Exactly. So don't be too disappointed if your cousin doesn't show up. They might be on their way to check out Wyoming."

"If only a job would open up on your crew at Crazy Horse."

"Last time that happened was six years ago. Don't look so gloomy. I could be all wrong. They might show up this afternoon."

We got up on the roof and patched the hole. By midmorning we had it done. It was a typically glorious bluesky day, and my dad proposed a bike ride. We'd been doing thirty or so miles every Sunday. The bike helped him to keep flexible. The work at Crazy Horse was awful hard on his body.

I passed on the bike ride, on account of how I didn't want to miss Quinn in case he showed up. My dad understood.

onto the front porch and down the steps into the sunshine. I was going to shoot some hoops to kill time. I set the space rock down among the granite river rocks that outline my mom's flower beds, then sat on the porch steps and pulled on my sneakers. As I was tying my shoes, I felt something I'd never felt before, a slight vibration running through me like a mild electric shock. It was so subtle I could barely feel it, but it was there. It ran from my scalp to the tips of my toes.

The phone rang. I ran for it, sure it would be Quinn.

It was my mom checking in from Iowa. We talked about the meteorite at first. As soon as she figured out that Dad was on a bike ride and I hadn't gone with him, she asked, all concerned, "Did you have an asthma episode?"

I didn't know why she even asked. At home, they're rare. We don't have dogs or cats. Pine pollen gives me a little trouble in June, but this was August. And she knew how touchy I was when anybody suggested I was anything but normal and couldn't do stuff on account of my asthma.

"No way," I said.

I could hear her wheels turning. She knew how into my bike I was, and riding with my dad on Sundays. Something had to be going on.

"Is something wrong?" she asked.

That's when I had to cough it up. I told her I was waiting for Quinn to arrive. "It's not a sure thing," I said, "just an outside possibility."

"Hmmm. If Quinn does come, and you two are hanging out . . . I'll be gone two weeks, and your dad will be at work . . . Just remember . . ."

"Remember what, Mom?"

"You know, take care of yourself. Cool it on the extreme stuff, okay?"

"And wear my helmet. No problem, Mom."

"Did Attila come across the bridge yesterday?"

The bridge my mom was talking about was the footbridge over Spring Creek. The forest service built it a long time ago. It's part of the hiking trail up the creek on the narrow strip of Black Hills National Forest that separates our place from the Carvers'.

Attila was the Carvers' Turkish war dog.

"Haven't seen hide nor hair of him," I reported.

"This isn't a good development, Attila coming across the bridge and onto our place."

"I'll tell him to beat it if he comes around."

"From a safe distance, I hope."

"You bet."

We signed off. Attila was on a strange tear, all right. There was no telling what had gotten into his head. He'd been stealing the river rocks from the border of my mom's flower beds. It was crazy. They had to weigh four or five pounds, and they were more than a mouthful, even for a Goliath of a dog like him. Three times, my mother had seen him steal one.

We were hoping Attila would just quit. Dealing with the Carvers was tricky, and we didn't like to rattle their cage. They were extremely territorial, and they outnumbered us forty acres to two. Their forty was fenced with barbed wire, and Attila patrolled the perimeter a couple of times a day. He'd never come through the fence until recently, when he started marauding for rocks.

I was curious what he wanted them for, but not curious enough to follow him home and find out. Attila was okay if you came onto the place with one of the Carver boys, but approach the fence without an escort and he would go ballistic.

The Carvers had three kids, all boys. Cal, the oldest, would be starting senior year in a few weeks. He'd gotten his driver's license back at the beginning of the summer after spending most of his junior year on probation, ineligible for football. What a catastrophe that had been, for the whole town. Cal had made all-state his sophomore year and was Hill City's hope for a championship.

Buzz and Max were identical twins. They were going to be freshmen in a few weeks, same as me. We'd been classmates since forever. It must've been third grade when they announced at school that they'd just gotten a Turkish war dog puppy. My dad looked up Turkish war dogs on his computer to see what we were up against. "Turkish war dog" turned out to be another name for the Anatolian shepherd. They're sheepdogs from Turkey.

It's a shame Attila didn't have a flock of sheep to protect. Even his spiked collar was just for show. At school, I'd asked Buzz what the collar was all about. He said it gave an advantage fighting wolves to the death. The wolf can't grab hold of the dog's throat.

As everybody knows, there aren't any wolves in the Black Hills, not to mention grizzly bears or even black bears. There used to be, but they were all killed out.

I'd asked Buzz why they were called "war dogs." Back in Turkey, he explained, they were used in combat for centuries. "It would have been cool," Max chimed in, "if they'd been in the Black Hills during the time of the pioneers. They coulda used 'em against the Sioux."

The Carver boys came up with this kind of stuff just to get my goat. Even though they never said so, it stuck in their craw that my dad worked at Crazy Horse. The whole Carver family was against the mountain statue of the Sioux chief, and everybody knew it.

Unfortunately, I had a thing about *their* dad, too, not that I ever made a peep about it. But I was around the twins a lot, and they could sense the fear.

I couldn't help it. Their dad was the coroner of Custer County, and ever since the day at school when some kids told me about him doing autopsies, what that meant, I haven't been able to keep certain images out of my head. In fact, my worst nightmare has to do with me and the Carvers' father, and you can guess what he's doing to me. I've never been able to shake it. Carver, what a perfectly nice name, but attach it to somebody who dissects people for a living, and it makes pictures in your mind. Or is it just me?

Quinn says I think too much. He's right about that. Let's leave it at this: the Carver twins and I had a very complicated relationship. If I make it sound like we were enemies, that's overdoing it. Over the years, I've messed around with them a lot, especially when Quinn's around. We weren't enemies and we weren't friends. Right below the surface there was always tension, and it went both ways.

Enough of that. I sailed out the front door intending to shoot some hoops, and there was Attila, on the driveway, with my meteorite in his jaws.

Across the Barbed Wire

ATTILA'S BEADY BROWN EYES stared at me without a trace of fear as his tail curled menacingly up and over his back. The war dog was as big as a Great Pyrenees but more slender and sculpted, all muscle, with a shorter, rougher coat. His muzzle, eyebrows, and ears were black. The rest of him was the color of dusty dirt.

"Take any other rock you want, Attila." I was trying my best to sound friendly and calm. "Just not that one."

A growl rumbled from under that spiked collar. Attila was only twenty feet away from where I stood on the porch. He seemed to be waiting to see what I would do.

How was I going to get him to drop my meteorite? Maybe throw something, startle him?

My eyes went to the hummingbird feeder, barely out

of reach. Unhook it, heave it at him?

Another growl. The beast could see exactly what I was thinking.

It was Attila who made the next move. Tail still curled over his back, he turned and ambled for home with my treasure in his mouth.

All I could do was follow. He was headed straight for the footbridge over the creek. Somehow I had to stop him before he got across.

I broke into a run. So did he.

I couldn't let him out of my sight. He might drop the meteorite where I'd never find it again.

In a flash, the thief was on the bridge. "Drop it!" I yelled, rattling the boards as I chased after him. "Drop it, Attila!"

The war dog ran up the far bank and into the woods, then paused for a glance back.

I stopped dead in my tracks. If I didn't chase, maybe he wouldn't run.

Wrong. He turned and bolted.

Attila was nearing the fence. In a few seconds he was going to be behind the barbed wire and on his home ground, which he was trained to protect.

I tried yelling at the top of my lungs. It didn't faze him. Agile as a deer, powerful as a grizzly, Attila bounded over the barbed wire. He trotted a ways, stopped, then turned around and waited. It looked like he was waiting to see if I was demented enough to follow.

Every hundred feet or so along their fence, the

Carvers had their property posted. The sign in front of me announced,

NO TRESPASSING
VIOLATORS WILL BE PROSECUTED

The last word had been crossed out, with the word DISMEMBERED hand-printed underneath. That would be Max, I thought.

I hesitated, my chest heaving with adrenaline and with something else. Here it was again, that strange head-to-toe electric current I'd felt earlier. I didn't know what was going on, but I couldn't worry about it now.

I'd never gone through their fence before. When you went to the Carvers', you approached up their driveway. You rang their doorbell.

If I ran back to the house, I could call them up or I could jump on my bike and go over there fast as I could. Probably they'd be home, at least Cal would. All summer there'd been banging and clanking coming from their place, which I figured was Cal working on one of his muscle cars. The oldest brother was quite the mechanic and welder.

Forget about calling or ringing the doorbell, I told myself. Either way, I'd lose track of Attila. Not only that, the Carvers would get curious about the rock. If they hadn't seen the fireball last night, they would've heard about it by now.

I didn't have any choice. I had to stay with Attila and keep my eye on the prize.

I bellied under the fence. As I got to my feet on the other side, Attila was still standing there in the trees, no more than forty feet away, the space traveler in his drooling jaws. He tensed. He growled.

"C'mon, Attila," I crooned. "You know who I am. You wouldn't hurt me, would you? That's my rock you've got, and you were out of bounds when you took it. Be a nice war dog and drop it, okay?"

My adversary wagged his tail, very slightly.

Was he trying to draw me in a little closer before he tore me to shreds, or was he actually feeling playful?

There was no telling.

Attila turned and trotted for home.

I hesitated, then gave chase through the pines. After a minute I glimpsed the big meadow ahead, the huge clearing behind the Carvers' log house. Attila was nearly there. No doubt he would sprint for home once he was out of the trees.

He didn't. At the edge of the grass, the war dog turned around and waited for me to catch up. What now? I wondered, heaving for breath.

Attila did exactly what I'd been hoping for all along. He dropped the meteorite. He dropped it and sat behind it, even wagged his tail.

He wanted to play. Wanted me to come and get it. "Good boy," I said. "That's right, we've been buddies for years."

Soon as I tried to take a step closer, that growl started up again.

Drawn to something beyond, my eyes left the dog. From where I was standing, just inside the trees, I couldn't see the Carvers' house but I could see to the far end of the meadow.

There was some kind of giant metal contraption down there, so huge it couldn't possibly be real. *What in the world?* I had to blink and look again.

Unbelievable! All that clanking and banging I'd been hearing . . . The Carver boys had been building a catapult all summer, a war machine from the Dark Ages like the scale model Buzz and Max had made in school, only this one was actual size!

When the time was right I would tell them I'd discovered their colossal secret and ask for a demonstration. My eyes went back to the rock thief. I edged closer. "C'mon, Attila."

Another growl was what I was expecting. Instead, Attila backed away from the meteorite and sat down again, about five feet back.

Come and get it, he seemed to be saying. Make my day.

That buzzing, I was feeling it again. Everything tingling and electrical. It seemed to add to my hyper-alertness. I felt so focused I could've counted every hair in Attila's dark muzzle.

I stepped closer, feeling the pine needles under my feet. Attila rose to all fours, tensed like a trap about to spring, and started barking.

Barking his head off.

I froze in my tracks.

From where I stood, the meteorite was a whole lot closer to the war dog than to me. For all the barking, he wasn't taking his eye off me, wasn't about to be surprised.

I better figure this out pretty quick, I thought. The Carvers were going to come running, and there was no way they were going to let me go home with my meteorite, even if I told them how it had come down on our place, into my bedroom. I could hear one of their favorite expressions right now: "Possession is nine tenths of the law."

The barking kept up, and over it I heard shouts. Max and Buzz were on their way. I could see them running full bore, yelling something I couldn't make out. They might be entering high school, but they were as fast and aggressive as NFL linebackers, and nearly as big. With me back in the trees, the twins couldn't tell who it was, but they knew they had a trespasser dead to rights.

I don't know what got into me. No matter how many pieces they had to carry me to the hospital in, I wasn't giving up what was mine.

I flew at that rock like a guided missile. Just coiled and flew. As lightning-fast as the dog was, it should have been impossible, but somehow I pounced faster and beat him to it. I pulled the traveler into my body, curled into a ball, and hung on for dear life, that snapping and snarling war dog all over me.

5

You Gotta Be Mental

I F NOT FOR BUZZ'S COMMAND—*"Leave it!"*—shouted at the top of his lungs, I might've been mauled to unrecognizable shreds. As it was, the war dog kept pummeling me and snarling bloody murder until the twins got there. I stole a glance from my fetal position and found Max standing over me. Buzz was pulling Attila back by that spiked collar. It was all he could do to pull the dog off me.

"Are you out of your mind?" Max screamed. "He could've torn you apart! You idiot, Steele, what were you doing?"

Attila was barking his head off and lunging to break free of Buzz's grip. "Leave it!" Buzz commanded again, and the war dog finally began to chill.

"Well, Steele?" Max, the older one by half an hour,

with the tight, curly black hair, always called me by my last name.

"You can get up now, Brady," said Buzz. His real name was Bernard, but he'd always gone by Buzz, after his haircut. "Answer Max's question."

My chest was heaving so bad, I couldn't even speak. I got to my knees.

"Must be his asthma," said Max, and I hoped he wasn't right. All that dog dander I'd had in my face could trigger an attack bad enough to send me to the emergency room, and I'd left home without my inhaler. How could I have been so stupid?

Max looked disgusted. "Got your inhaler?"

I shook my head as I finally reached my feet. "It's at home," I managed.

"Dumb," Max said. I was kind of holding my meteorite against my side, hoping they wouldn't notice it.

Stealthy as a mountain lion, Attila had crept back into play without any of us noticing. With a slap of a paw, he knocked the space rock out of my hand, grabbed it, and ran off with it.

Fortunately he didn't run far, just a short ways into the meadow. The war dog turned around and looked at the twins. He seemed to be waiting for instructions, but they were baffled. Maybe they were figuring I'd grabbed the rock for self-defense, but that wouldn't explain why I was trespassing.

I was sick, just sick. Do something, I thought. "That rock's mine," I blurted out. "I mean, it's my mom's.

26

Attila's been stealing rocks from around her flower beds. She called from Iowa this morning and told me to make sure he didn't take any more rocks."

Smirkers from birth, Max and Buzz thought this was pretty funny. "Really," I insisted.

Buzz cracked up. "We told him to get rocks, we just didn't know how far he was going to get them. We've got a big pile going. We're going to throw them with our medieval siege weapon."

"I saw it just now, your catapult, like the one you made for school, except—"

"Except this one's the real deal," Buzz said proudly. "What do you think of it, Brady?"

"It's the most amazing thing I ever saw. Does it work?"

"It's not done, but we're close," Max put in. "It's top secret, Steele."

"In that case I won't tell anybody. Is it okay if I tell Quinn?"

The twins were big fans of Quinn. Whenever he'd come down from Lead, they always invited us over for paintball. "War games," they called it. Them against us, two hours of furious action chasing each other around their forty acres with guns. They even provided the cammo outfits, the goggles, and the paintball guns. Those guys always gave better than they got, but even if you only splattered them once or twice, it felt mighty good.

"Quinn comin' this summer?" asked Max. He had a

growl to his voice even when he wasn't growling.

"Maybe today."

"In that case you can tell him about our siege cata-pult, but if word gets out, you guys won't get to see our demo. Invited guests only. We'll let you know."

"Bring a toilet," Buzz chimed in. "We're collecting a lot of cool things to throw. Hey, did you see the meteor shower last night?"

Uh-oh, I thought. Be careful, Brady. These guys are smart as whips. "I was watching TV," I said. "Missed it."

"We were in Rapid at a show."

"Well, I guess I'll head home."

"Go suck on your inhaler," snorted Max. Evidently he'd decided we were getting too friendly. Aside from the haircuts, the biggest difference between the twins was this: Buzz played at being mean, whereas Max really was. Max, especially, liked to keep me on edge. I stood there awkwardly.

"What are you waiting for, Steele?"

"The rock."

I glanced at their faces. Buzz was willing to let me have it, but Max wasn't so sure. "How can you prove this rock is yours?"

"That should be obvious if I went to the trouble."

"Too much trouble," Max said a little suspiciously. It looked like he was close to figuring it out.

Fortunately, he didn't quite get there. "You gotta be mental, Steele. Lemme get this straight. Attila had the rock, and you took it away from him? How'd that work?"

"It was all a blur, but I did."

"That was crazy."

"I know. I totally admit it."

The brothers exchanged shrugs, and told Attila to drop the rock. It took both of them. Attila was mighty unhappy about it, but finally he let it go.

Max handed it over. "Here's your stupid rock, Steele."

I made a beeline home. They were right about me being crazy. I'd lived through it in one piece, though, and was pumped to have the space traveler back.

6

A Strange Summer

BACK HOME, I SHOWERED off the dog smell and dressed in clean clothes. My dad wasn't back from his bike ride, but I could hear the crunch of wheels on gravel. A heavy vehicle was on its way up the driveway, a diesel from the sound of it. I grabbed up the traveler and bolted out the front door, thinking it might be my uncle's truck.

It was them, all right, in a cloud of dust. Uncle Jake had his motorcycle trailer in tow, and his Harley was on it.

Behind the pickup's windshield, my uncle and my cousin both looked different than they had when I saw them last. Uncle Jake had grown a beard. Quinn's hair was longer than I'd ever seen it, like he hadn't gotten it cut all summer. He was wearing a white T-shirt with big black letters. I couldn't make out what they said.

The diesel pulled onto the concrete apron in front of my dad's metal and wood shop. Quinn poured out of the passenger side, same old grin, fluid as ever but with more muscles. What his T-shirt said was GO BIG OR GO HOME. Quinn's eyes were on the meteorite. I held it up like a trophy.

Uncle Jake was hanging back, looking around the place fondly. "Cool," Quinn said as I handed over the rock.

I'd been expecting "extreme" or "insane."

"Heavy sucker," Quinn said, doing a few curls with it. "Looks like a baked potato."

"That's what *I* thought. Hey, you look like you've been working out, like with weights."

"You should be doing the same thing, for basketball."

"Dad says to wait another year."

Uncle Jake sidled over, reached out, and shook my hand. I told him I liked his new beard and ponytail. He laughed, kind of shrugged.

Uncle Jake said to Quinn, "Notice anything different about your cousin?"

"How could I miss it? I could stand in his shade."

"Yeah, right," I said. Uncle Jake wanted us to stand back to back, and we did.

"Exactly the same height," my uncle reported. "Brady's really shot up since Christmas."

"We'll see if it does him any good," Quinn cracked.

"I can probably dunk over him."

"You could if we lowered the rim a couple of feet and I played on my knees."

With a glance toward the house, Uncle Jake asked if my dad was home, and I brought him up to speed. I thought for sure he would wait around, but he was hot to jump on his Harley and ride up to Sturgis. He wanted to get in on the opening mayhem.

Sturgis sits just north of the Black Hills. The second week of August every year, it's home base for three hundred thousand bikers—biggest motorcycle rally in the world. This afternoon, there'd be a hundred thousand on Main Street. Next morning the bikers would head for the prairies, the Badlands, and the Pine Ridge Reservation, but mostly they'd ride the Black Hills. The following Sunday they would rendezvous back in Sturgis for the closing festivities, then blast home to who-knows-where.

"I've never ridden the whole enchilada before," Uncle Jake said, "only the weekends on either side."

"The mine never gave him much vacation time," Quinn explained. "He always saved what he had for doing stuff with me."

"Unemployment has its perks," Uncle Jake noted wryly.

"Don't believe him," Quinn said. "He can't stand it. He's totally a fish out of water."

"It's been a strange summer," Uncle Jake agreed. "Quinn's been the working man. As I've been telling him, he's the ant and I'm the grasshopper."

"Don't believe him, Brady. Dad makes it sound like he's been over at Deadwood making contributions to the casinos, when really he's been out looking for work."

"On the road?" I asked.

Uncle Jake shrugged. "Some, but mostly on the Internet. Saves gas. Hey, guys, I'm ready to pull on my leathers and kick it into gear."

"What about lunch, Uncle Jake? We can make tacos. You like tacos."

"We just ate in Hill City. Grabbed some sandwiches at the drive-through and ate in the park."

My head jerked in Quinn's direction. "The Grabba Java? You saw Crystal?"

"Barely," Quinn said. "My dad drove through on her mom's side."

"Awesome sandwiches, just like Quinn promised," Uncle Jake said. "I asked the lady if she had regular coffee, black. She said she only had espresso."

Quinn laughed. "Brady, you shoulda been there. Dad told Maggie that all that espresso lingo was way over his head, and he wasn't good at languages."

"Uncle Jake flirting with Maggie Ruiz, the most beautiful single woman in the Hills? This is good!"

"Are you kidding? He was just being himself."

"So, what happened next, Uncle Jake?"

"You're right about her being beautiful, Brady. She asked me if I'd ever had a designer coffee before, and all I could think was, I'd lived this long without buying a four-dollar coffee, so why start now? I told her . . . How did I put it, Quinn?"

"You said, 'I'm wary of investments, not ready to invest in coffee.' He actually said that, Brady. Can you believe it?"

"What then?"

"Dad turned red as a tomato."

"The last thing on my mind was insulting her, and I just had."

"My dad, the smooth operator. Right then Crystal looked over and spotted me—she was in between customers. 'Hi, Quinn!'—big smile."

"You lucky dog."

"She told her mom who I was. Then Crystal said, 'This must be your dad.'"

"Quinn admitted that I was. That was generous of you, son."

"Then what, Uncle Jake?"

"Along with our sandwiches and Quinn's soda, the lady handed me the tallest cup of coffee I've ever seen. I was about to tell her she must have gotten confused, but I held off. I was confused myself. 'On the house,' she said. 'Looks like you're on your way to Sturgis—can't have Quinn's dad driving drowsy.'"

"Sounds like Maggie," I said.

"Dad made a decent recovery. He asked Maggie what she just gave him, in case he was going to come by and ask for one again."

"What was it called, son?"

"Triple-shot vanilla latte—three shots of fine-ground premium espresso coffee with steamed milk and a little vanilla flavor."

"I'll have to admit, it sure was good. Mighty good. I'm going to be the most alert biker in Sturgis tonight—practically took my head off. Well, you guys aren't going to miss me unless I do something about leaving the premises."

Uncle Jake parked his truck alongside my dad's shop. Quinn hopped onto the trailer and handed down his mountain bike and then his road bike. He hadn't forgotten his panniers. Whenever he visited, we always did at least one overnight ride.

While we were grabbing Quinn's duffel bag, sleeping bag, and such from the crew cab, Uncle Jake off-loaded his Harley. Then he pulled on his leather jacket, chaps, and motorcycle boots. It wasn't long before he was mounted and ready to turn the key. "It's been nice seeing you, Brady. Tell your dad I'll have a good visit with him when I get back. We have a lot of catching up to do. You guys have a good time messin' around, okay?"

"Guaranteed," Quinn replied.

Uncle Jake fired up his gleaming machine. He gave a nod toward the rock in my hand. "All that talk about fancy coffee, and I forgot to make a fuss about your meteorite, and how happy I am that you're still with us. Are you going to check it out, find out if it's valuable in addition to being incredible?"

"I didn't think of that, but good idea!"

Driving out in black leather, on his silver and black Harley, Uncle Jake looked like a movie star. He was a good-looking guy to begin with, but with his new beard and ponytail, he looked like he should be on the Sturgis poster.

I said to Quinn, "How come your dad never wears a helmet? What if he ever got in an accident?"

Quinn shrugged. "I know what you mean. I have to, but he doesn't. I'm pretty sure it's because he can't stand helmet hair."

7

Bring Me Your Serious

QUINN THREW HIS DUFFEL bag on his bed, across the room from mine, then gave a close inspection to the puncture in the ceiling above my bed and the hole through my mattress. His pronouncement was worth waiting for: "That's so sick, it's wack."

A couple minutes later we were shooting hoops on the paved apron in front of my dad's shop, which is what we always did as soon as Quinn came down from Lead. Both of us played on school teams and were more than decent. There wasn't much doubt we'd both be JV starters in ninth grade.

We tossed our T-shirts aside and launched into a furious game of one-on-one. Quinn had always had a step on me. With his new strength to go along with his speed and quickness, I knew he'd be better than ever.

At the first opportunity, he faked me out in typical Quinn fashion, blew right by like my feet were buried in concrete. He scored with a reverse left-handed lay-in just to serve notice he'd been working on some new moves. He flipped me the ball. "Wake up, Brady. Bring your A game—I'm not taking any prisoners."

Kids from Lead are competitive to begin with, and tough as mining hammers and drills. Then there's Quinn. The only reason I was any good came from playing against him in the summers.

Five minutes in, we were drenched with sweat. The pace was unforgiving, and he had me down 16–12. I was keeping it as close as I could have expected. I mean, I'd never beaten him, and never really believed I would or could.

How I envied his new muscles, in his shoulders and arms especially, even his neck. There was no hope I was going to turn the tables on him.

Quinn scored with a couple of his sudden, silky outside jumpers, then blew by me again and took it to the hoop. "28–16," he announced, and tossed me the ball. "Bring it, Brady. Let's see what you got."

I dribbled in place, letting us both grab some of that thin Black Hills air. Our place on Spring Creek is nearly a mile high. I felt the strange electricity again, head to toe, and with it I felt a surge of strength pour through me. I wasn't breathing nearly as hard as I should have been. "Are you ready to play some serious basketball?" I said with a laugh.

"Oh, I see, you were only warming up. Bring me your serious."

Surprise him, I thought. Don't hold anything back.

And I didn't. I kept my eyes on my cousin's, accelerated on a dime, faked him left, faked him right, then went up for a jump shot, surprising myself with how high I was going, higher than I'd ever been. My release was effortless and smooth, and I drained it dead center, nothing but net. What a sweet, sweet sound.

Quinn's eyes were big. "Where did that come from?"

"No idea," I replied. I got ready to defend. "Game on," I told him.

Quinn was ready to step it up a notch himself. "Comin' through," he announced, which may or may not have been true. He drove for the basket, long hair flying, but I didn't buy his fakes. For whatever reason, I still had that lightning quickness that had enabled me to beat Attila to the punch. I picked Quinn clean, then spun and scored with a left-handed reverse of my own. I've always been awkward with my left hand, but it felt totally natural.

"Beautiful," Quinn said, more than a little shaken. "You go to basketball camp this summer?"

"Nah, I've just been playin' against my dad."

Not even very much, I thought, but I wasn't going to say it. Mostly I'd been hanging out at the town swimming pool.

I flipped Quinn the ball. He looked more determined than ever, but I suffocated him with defense. When he finally went up for a shot, I didn't allow him an open look, and it clanked off the rim. I soared for the rebound and banked it through while I was hanging in midair. Quinn was looking at me like he wasn't even sure this was me.

Before long we were tied. Soon after that, for the first time in my life, I not only pulled ahead, I put him away. With me leading by fourteen, Quinn called it quits.

"Incredible," he said. "What got into you?"

"No idea. Feelin' my oats, I guess."

"Wish I was eating out of the same feed bag." Quinn looked kind of stunned. What had just happened didn't compute. And the same went for me.

My cousin didn't stay stunned for very long. Quinn was still Quinn, his mind going as fast as his body. "Remember that time we played egg toss? How about meteorite toss, on the lawn, only fast, more like hot potato?"

We started at about ten feet, underhanding the rock to each other from farther and farther apart. Catching the thing was fairly brutal. Before long we were forty feet apart, neither of us having dropped the spud. This time, instead of giving it plenty of loft, Quinn did a full under-handed windup and delivered a screaming fastball.

Like a dope, I tried to catch it. Game over. The heel of my thumb hurt insanely. Quinn came running. "You shoulda let it go by!"

"Thought I could make the catch."

"Lemme see."

"Look, it's just a scrape."

"Yeah, but it's bleeding."

"Not hardly." I was pretty good at shaking off pain. "The main thing is, I made the catch."

I washed the scrape with the garden hose. The bleeding had pretty much quit. We drank from the hose and splashed the meteorite to make it glisten. Quinn held it in his palm and said, "Think where it's been."

"I know. He's a real space traveler."

"He? Are you going to give him a name?"

I thought for a second. "How about Fred?"

"Fred? Why Fred?"

"I dunno, I just like it."

"Maybe the letters stand for something?"

"How about . . . 'Far Roaming Earth Diver.'"

"There you go. Fred is perfect. Welcome to our planet, Fred."

Next thing I knew Quinn was bouncing around, tossing Fred between his hands, off-the-wall excited. "Just think how valuable Fred might be! I mean, he's from outer space! We have to find out!"

"I've been thinking we should take him to the museum in Hill City. Tomorrow's Monday; they'll be open."

"Great idea. That meteorite expert guy will probably be there, the one the TV station talked to. *All right*, things are moving right along!"

We made ourselves some nachos in the toaster oven. As we devoured them, I filled Quinn in on the medieval war machine the Carvers were building in their back-yard. He was happy all over again that he'd quit his job busing dishes. I swore him to secrecy, of course.

I didn't explain about my trespassing episode. He knew Attila. It would have defied explanation. Every summer Quinn had tried to make friends with Attila, and every time he'd struck out. Deep in his genes, the war dog knew that everybody outside of his family was on his enemies list.

"Sure hope they get their catapult finished while I'm around," Quinn said. "This, I gotta see."

Quinn wondered if Cal was going to play football his senior year, after losing a season on probation. "I sure think so," I said. "Football practice starts next week, and everybody's counting on it. The rest of the league better watch out. Cal's going to come back with a vengeance. With the famous Bolt from the Blue carrying the football and his huge little brothers blocking for him, the Rangers are going to go places. The town's talking title. State title."

"Buzz and Max are a lock for varsity freshman year?"

"Unless they break into the school and trash stuff, I guess."

"Cal did that about this time a year ago, right?"

"Yeah, at two in the morning, after a party. Cal and that other player were beered up."

"Buzz and Max will stay out of trouble, would be my bet."

"Mine, too. They have too much to lose. The newspaper gave 'em nicknames last month—Buzz Saw and Max Hurt. Called 'em the future of Hill City football. So, what are you up for next, like today?"

Quinn had a glint in his eye. "Monster bike ride."

"I'm ready. My legs feel like pistons in a Porsche."

"Are your lungs good to go?"

"Like bellows at a steel mill. What about doing a loop? Iron Mountain, Custer State Park, and back via Needles Highway?"

"That would be a monster, all right. I'll drop you on Iron Mountain like you've never been dropped. Leave you eating my exhaust like I'm on a Harley and you're on a tricycle."

"We'll see about that. I need some fuel, though. What do you say we head over to Crystal's for sandwiches and smoothies?"

8

Crystal

WE LEFT A NOTE FOR my dad, then jumped on our road bikes. Our mountain bikes would get their chance another day.

From home to Hill City normally takes twenty minutes on the Mickelson Trail, the rails-to-trails bike path that runs the length of the Black Hills. We did it in fifteen. It was one of those perfect Black Hills days, deep blue sky and dry mountain air scented by ponderosa pine.

The Mickelson Trail continued along Spring Creek, but we got off it and pedaled into town. Hill City sits halfway between the mountain carvings, Rushmore and Crazy Horse. It got its start as a mining camp during the 1876 gold rush. Its boom went bust when word came of nuggets big as candy bars being found to the north in Deadwood Gulch.

We rolled past the sign that says, HILL CITY, HEART OF THE HILLS, POPULATION 800 PEOPLE, ONE OLD TRAIN, AND FIFTEEN DINOSAUR SKELETONS AND SKULLS. As we waited to cross the main street, we could hear the steam whistle of *The 1880*, the train that takes the tourists eleven miles over to Rushmore. Traffic was heavy with the usual RVs and swarms of bikers roaring north to Sturgis.

Downtown is about eight blocks long. We walked our bikes along the sidewalk on the west side of Main underneath the hanging flower baskets and past the art galleries, gift shops, and restaurants.

"Trendier than ever," Quinn said. "I can't help myself. I like it."

A few blocks past the museum, we headed for Crystal's window at the Grabba Java.

We were fifth in line. It was one o'clock, still prime time for the legions of fans addicted to the hearty bean ground and brewed by the famous Magdalena "Maggie" Ruiz.

Even at the height of tourist season, half of Maggie's business came from locals. Crystal's mom even did a good business in winter. Her smile and personality were so magical, there were stories of Mormons driving through, buying four-dollar coffee, then throwing it in the first trash can they came to. It didn't hurt that Maggie was beautiful and single.

By now we'd moved up to third. Quinn asked if Crystal and her mom were still living out of town at the

Creekside. I told him they were. The Creekside was a string of cabins on the opposite side of town from us, on Spring Creek as it flowed north toward Sheridan Lake.

Finally, our turn.

Crystal's smile lit up, and she let it shine. "What's up, Brady? Hey, Quinn! I haven't seen you since a couple of hours ago. I was afraid you weren't going to show up this summer."

"Glad I did," Quinn said.

Crystal took our orders and got to work putting together our smoothies. The sandwiches were premade. "You guys see the meteor shower last night?"

"Show her, Brady."

I slung my daypack off my back and pulled out the space traveler. "Meet Fred. Fred arrived at my house last night."

"Fred? Is that really a meteorite? How'd you find him?"

"He pretty much found me." I filled her in on a few of the nearly gruesome details but had to cut it short. People were waiting behind us, and time was at a premium.

Crystal poured our smoothies out of their blenders into tall to-go cups, lidded them, and popped in the straws. My bike was closest to the window, and I took them one by one from her hands. I handed Quinn his smoothie and glanced back at Crystal. Her long, raven-black hair had a sheen to it that seemed miraculous. Quinn was bumping my shoulder, trying to distract me with something. He was handing me a twenty. Somehow I'd forgotten this whole exchange had anything to do with money. I passed it along to Crystal.

"Keep the change," Quinn said.

"Hey, thanks." Crystal beamed, and handed out our sandwiches. "That was cool meeting your dad, Quinn. What a guy!"

"I'm sure he made quite an impression on your mom."

"How's that? She didn't say anything."

"Nothing about his foot in his mouth?"

"Not at all. When he came through the second time, on his Harley, he looked so cool—"

"He came back?"

"Yeah, to get a sandwich for the road, came to my window. He knew how jammed the restaurants would be up in Sturgis."

I shouldn't have looked over my shoulder. The guy right behind us, a biker, gave me a scowl that could have corroded titanium. That was one scary-looking character. We said good-bye to Crystal and started to walk our bikes over to Grabba Java's picnic tables. "Hey, Quinn," she called. "I like your hair!"

Quinn tossed his head a little, opened his mouth for a quick comeback, but settled for a flustered wave. I made like I didn't notice.

"Cool that your dad came back to Grabba Java," I said as we sat down and started in on the sandwiches. "He should've come through Maggie's side, though, and flirted with her some more."

"Not gonna happen. Anybody he starts to get interested in, next thing I know he runs the other way. My theory is he thinks there can't be anyone to measure up to my mother."

"My parents say she was awful special, your mom."

"I know. Everybody says that. I wish I could remember her . . ."

"So tell me about Wyoming. Your dad's looking at work in the gas fields over there?"

"Yeah, at twenty-one dollars an hour, in the Jonah field."

"You might really move there?"

"I'm afraid so."

"He's already gone over and checked it out?"

"We both did, a couple of weeks ago."

"Isn't Yellowstone over there somewhere?"

"Not close enough."

"So, what's it like?"

"A total wasteland. Dustiest place I've ever seen, and the wind blows hard all the time. My dad has a line on a fifty-year-old trailer somebody's been using for storage. It's totally a piece of junk and the rent they want for it is unbelievable. They're punching gas wells like crazy over there, and all these guys from Michigan are pouring in for the jobs. I guess they used to be autoworkers. Anyway, my dad had to put a thousand bucks nonrefundable on the trailer so they'd save it for him, even though he's still undecided about the whole deal. At least he says he is."

"Sounds bleak."

"Bleak is the word."

"Sure hope he doesn't have to go through with it."

"It looks like he will. We've got a 'For Sale' sign in front of our house in Lead."

"You could stay behind and live with us."

"I think my dad's going to talk to your dad about it after Sturgis."

"That'd be awesome."

"I guess."

"You guess? We could start high school together, play basketball together, flip a coin over who asks Crystal out . . . She likes your hair, dude."

Quinn popped me one on the arm. "You're such a fungus, Brady. Let's buy some water and some Gatorade, a couple of PowerBars, check our inflation, and blast off on that ride. Sort out who gets dropped and who does the dropping."

9

You Were an Animal

I T TOOK US NO TIME at all to blast over to Keystone, ten miles east with a lot of downhill. I led the way, which was unusual. Quinn was the stronger rider, and I'd always let him draft me. The guy out front is working so much harder, there's no comparison.

Whatever was going on, I had never felt stronger. With a look over my shoulder, I knew exactly what Quinn was thinking: it was brainless of me to go out in front on these first ten easy miles to Keystone. Once we started up the Iron Mountain Road, I wouldn't have anything left. He would drop me like a rock off the Empire State Building.

What did I care? It wouldn't be anything new. I had this amazing feeling that the sky was the limit. Who knows, maybe I could turn the tables on him twice in one day.

We pulled into Keystone, which is just around the corner from Rushmore. Its boardwalk was jam-packed with tourists flocking to the T-shirt shops and burger places. We rode side by side through town, sucking from our water bottles. I wasn't even breathing hard. I couldn't believe it. I felt like an iron man. "Wanna stop for a rest?" I asked.

I guess it came out like I was offering to go easy on him. Quinn shot me a look like I'd never seen from him before. "Not unless you do."

"Alrighty, then."

It took only a couple minutes to breeze through Keystone. When I hung a left onto the beginning of the Iron Mountain Road and started to climb, I glanced at Quinn and saw fire in his eyes. I was in for some serious humility training.

I put my head down and went to work. This scenic byway, narrow and winding, was a big draw for tourists, and this was Sturgis week. In addition to the cars, SUVs, pickups, and RVs, motorcycles were flying by like squadrons of hornets. I kept my front wheel safely on the white shoulder line. By now Quinn should have been breathing down my neck, but I couldn't hear him at all. With the first tunnel in sight, I looked back. Amazingly, he was a hundred yards behind.

He's only playing with you, I thought. Still thinks you're going to burn out anytime now. He's waiting for the steepest grade, and then he's going to blow by. Drop you like you're standing as still as a ton of bricks that slid off the back of a truck.

Can't let that happen, I vowed as I passed through the cool of the tunnel. On the far side I stood up on my pedals and really pushed. Maybe I could open up an even wider lead.

The gears I was using weren't as low as I usually had to go to. My heart was pumping like a steam engine. My muscles felt like iron, my tendons like cables of steel. That strange electrical buzz was running through me all the way to my grip on the handlebars.

Climbing all the while, I was about to enter a big sweeping corner. I took another look and found Quinn even farther back, two hundred yards at least. He had his head down and was working hard. Quinn wasn't used to this. What was going through his mind?

As the corner straightened out, I saw three riders up ahead decked out in identical Lycra outfits of orange, white, and neon green. They were attacking the grade like they were taking no prisoners. Probably they were training for a race.

For a while I held my position, breathing deeper while wondering if it might be possible to reel them in. It would have been more fun for Quinn and me to both try to pass these guys, but Quinn had fallen back some more.

Wouldn't that be something, I thought, if I could catch these serious riders, these Lycra guys? Probably they were from a competitive cycling club. For all I knew, they were pro racers.

Go for it, I thought, and began my attack. I put my head down, kept pumping hard. Incredibly, I kept gaining on them. As I got close, approaching the second tunnel, I checked to see if there was any traffic trying to overtake the four of us. There wasn't. I swung out wide and put the hammer down as I climbed up one of the famous pigtails, where the Iron Mountain Road actually passes over itself. My burst of speed placed me alongside the three. The Lycra guys were in their twenties. They were lean, mean bicycling machines.

I stood on the pedals long enough to regain the white line in front of them. The mountain was dishing out the pain, all right, but I had something left. I opened up a gap in front of the trio.

What a feeling! It was like I'd broken through some threshold and come out on the other side. It was like I'd never had a problem with my lungs. They felt as big as a whale's. Now I wanted to see if I could keep pushing like this all the way to the top. No letting the Lycra guys catch me.

As I approached the tunnel, I had a great view almost straight down to where I'd been shortly before. I looked for Quinn, but he wasn't there yet.

The road bent south again, climbing another pigtail toward the last tunnel. From behind, another pack of Sturgis riders roared by, all thunder and chrome and black leather. The grade was brutally steep. With the summit tunnel in sight, I stood on the pedals and let it rip. This one was going to go in the record books.

Riding through that last tunnel, I was on top of the world. On the other side, I jumped off the bike and took in the awesome view to the south with the green, rolling prairies meeting the mountains. Then I looked back from where I'd come and found the Lycra guys emerging from the tunnel. As they coasted by, the lead rider bobbed his head in my direction. "Strong rider," he called.

Strong rider! He was talking about me!

A pickup with a slide-in camper squeezed through the tunnel, then a rumbling swarm of motorcycles, but no sign yet of Quinn. The view north through the tunnel is an American classic, just the way the engineers planned it. The tunnel frames the faces of the Rushmore presidents perfectly, bright white granite surrounded by deep green forest and blue, blue sky.

If you live in the Hills, you think about those four a lot. In my book, Abraham Lincoln has to be the greatest, but Theodore Roosevelt will always be my favorite.

T.R. knew and loved the Black Hills, and not only that, he had a scary time with asthma as a kid before the medicines in my inhaler were even dreamed of. After he was president, T.R. went on an expedition to South America to explore a tributary of the Amazon that had never even been mapped. He ran into piranhas, starvation, rapids, malaria, mutiny, and Indians with poison-tipped arrows. Talk about extreme and insane. He lived to tell the tale, even if his health was broken.

Right here, right now, I felt closer to Teddy Roosevelt than ever before. I murmured those heroic lines of his I had memorized in fifth grade: "Far better it is to dare mighty things, to win glorious triumphs, even though checkered by failure, than to take rank with those poor spirits who neither enjoy much nor suffer much, because they live in the gray twilight that knows not victory nor defeat."

Here came Quinn at last, maybe five minutes behind me. Five minutes was incomprehensible. Had he been dogging it? Was he feeling sick? What was going on?

Quinn got off his bike and joined me on a big granite boulder with a drop-dead view of the prairies of Custer State Park. No gloating, I told myself. Quinn didn't have much to say. We drank Gatorade and chewed our sticky PowerBars. He looked more wasted than I'd ever seen him. Finally he came out with "What was that all about?"

"What do you mean?"

"Don't give me that, you Nerf ball. I'm talking about that climb you just did. I'm talkin' about what in the world's gotten into you?"

"Feelin' good, that's all."

"You were an animal."

"I can't account for it."

"At least tell me you had to honk on your inhaler. Did you put it away just before I limped in like a ground sloth?"

"I haven't had it out."

"Dude, you rule. Never thought I would see this happen."

Remembering my no-gloating rule, I changed the subject. "What a view, eh?"

Quinn didn't answer for a long time. I wasn't sure where his head was at. Finally he said, "You couldn't pry me out of the Black Hills with a crowbar."

Me neither, I thought. But Quinn might not have a choice. No wonder he seemed so far away.

I tightened my chin strap for the descent into Custer State Park. Quinn did the same.

10

Give Us Your T-shirt

WE FLEW DOWN THE mountain onto the prairie in Custer State Park and hung a right, to the west. Tourists were parked all along the shoulder taking pictures of a small herd of buffalo that had gotten out of the fence, which wasn't unusual. Some of the tourists were out of their cars and getting much too close. Hadn't they seen the yellow, diamond-shaped warnings posted every couple of miles along the road? They pictured a buffalo dumping a stick man head over heels.

"Check this out." Quinn was pointing to a man in shorts and a Hawaiian shirt. Snapping pictures as he went, the guy was walking up to a humongous buffalo bull that was lying down and chewing its cud. The tourist finally held up at about five yards but kept shooting as the bull rose to its feet—not a good sign. Didn't he know this was a wild animal?

We got off our bikes wondering if we were about to witness one of those incidents where a tourist gets flattened and stomped by two thousand pounds of bent-out-of-shape buffalo. They're unpredictable beasts, and can charge in a heartbeat. "Look out," Quinn called to the man in the flashy shirt. "Object through lens is closer than it might appear!"

The guy looked over at us all annoyed like we were being punks. He took another step, lifted the camera, took a few more pictures. Ominously, the bull swallowed its cud and lowered its massive head slightly. The guy turned his back like you might on a statue and ambled in the direction of his car, unscathed. As for the bull, it burped up its cud and went back to grinding the wad on its molars, but remained standing.

We were about to jump back on our bikes. "Uh-oh," Quinn said. "Monkey see, monkey do."

A little boy, disposable camera in hand, was wobbling toward the bull. The kid looked barely four, too young to be into extreme sports.

On he went, closer and closer, herky-jerky on his chubby little legs. Where were his parents?

The little photographer stopped exactly where the clueless tourist had, and he sighted through his viewfinder. The small eyes of the mountainous animal were locked on him like lasers. What was taking the kid so long to get a picture? The bull lowered his head and pawed the ground. Uh-oh.

By now a lot of the people watching from along the shoulder were alert to the impending catastrophe. Shouts and cries went up; people were pointing. "Somebody do something!" a woman wailed. Somebody had to, but nobody did until I took off at a dead sprint.

Running full out, I heard the bull snort, saw the blur of its charge. I got there a second before the animal's head and horns did, and I was able to scoop the kid out of the path of destruction.

The buffalo skidded to a stop and turned around to face me, mad as a one-ton hornet.

The monster trotted toward me, paused, lowered his head. From the side, someone came flying at me—the little boy's dad? The man grabbed the kid from my arms, spun, and ran as fast as he could. The bull chased after him, stopped short, let him go. Then the buffalo swung around and glared at me. He lowered his head and pawed the ground. It was me he wanted.

I darted to the left—he cut me off. I darted to the right—he cut me off. "Nice buffalo," I said, but there wasn't anything nice about him. The beast lowered his massive head to show me his sharp, curling horns. He was practically breathing fire.

And now he was charging. This much I knew for sure: if I turned and ran, I was history. The world's fastest human couldn't outrun one of these things.

The bull was closing so fast and so furiously, its thundering hoofs shook the earth. The enormous head and horns were tilted down like a battering ram, its angry tail sticking up like a stinger. A couple seconds was all I had. An idea popped into mind like a string of pictures. The thing to do was to run *toward* him instead of away from him.

I was going to have to time this just right. My eyes locked onto the wide crown of his skull. *Now!* I told myself, and charged the charging bull with three quick steps. Off the third step I bounded up and came down with both feet together like I was at the end of a diving board. As my knees uncoiled, I threw myself up and forward, way forward, hands outstretched and close together.

Barely before impact, I was airborne, and nearly upside down. I planted my hands on the base of the buffalo's horns and vaulted high as I could, tucking and tumbling in midair. The whole sickening length of the beast passed beneath me. Somehow I landed on two feet.

Quick as I could, I turned around to face the buffalo. He was whirling around, too.

Here he comes, I thought, but the storm in his buffalo brain had passed. The bull stood there a few seconds looking puzzled, then went off to join the herd.

I headed for Quinn at the side of the road. All the people standing around started to applaud. Then a bunch flocked toward me, taking pictures and stuff. One guy had his wallet out and was trying to give me a hundred-dollar bill. "You saved my kid! Here, take it!"

I brushed his hand aside, Quinn looking at me like I was crazy. By now there must've been fifty people crowding around, and I was getting claustrophobic. A couple of cute girls wanted me to pose with them. One said, "Could you, like, sign your T-shirt, and give it to me?"

"Let's get out of here," I said to Quinn from the side of my mouth, and took off. I grabbed my bike off the ground and swung aboard.

Quinn caught up as we passed by the famous Game Lodge where President Coolidge used to keep cool during the summertime. The shoulder there was extra wide, and Quinn was able to ride alongside. "That was nuts," he yelled, "start to finish."

"Insane," I agreed.

One of the cars going by slowed to our speed, and the windows came down. It was those girls again, leaning out of the windows with cameras. "You with the hair," one of them yelled. "Get out of the picture!"

They took pictures of me on my bike, then sped off shrieking toward Custer.

Quinn was riding at my side again. "Brady, you're a total stud!"

"Knock it off, Quinn." I stood on the pedals and raced in front of him. I was totally pumped. I couldn't believe what had happened back there.

Quinn caught up. "'Give us your T-shirt! Give us your T-shirt!'"

The shoulder was narrowing, and Quinn had to drop in behind me. We scorched the next few miles. "Stop, you lunatic!" he yelled finally, and I did.

In the shade of a big cottonwood, we sat and drank

some water. I felt myself calming down at last. "Vaulting over a buffalo," Quinn started in, "where'd you come up with that, Brady? You did a three-sixty, at least. You even stuck the landing!"

"I can almost remember . . . Oh yeah, it was from a library book."

"A library book, eh?"

"Yeah, I was doing a report on ancient Crete."

"Crete?"

"You know, the island in the Mediterranean. They had this sport that was like bullfighting, only different. It was more of an athletic contest. Instead of killing the bull, the idea was to grab it by the horns and vault over it."

"You read that, and you remembered it?"

"I was really into the illustrations."

"So that's supposed to explain everything?"

"I guess."

"No way! What were you thinking, trying to save that kid?"

"I wasn't thinking, I just reacted."

"You ran so fast you were a total blur. What's going on, Brady?"

"What are you talking about?"

"I'm talking about the way you ran circles around me with the basketball this morning, the way you attacked Iron Mountain like a Tour de France rider. Both of those were amazing enough. Okay, you saw the buffalo-vault deal in a book, but that doesn't explain how you were able to pull it off. What's going on, you goof-ball?"

"I wish I knew."

"How long has it been going on?"

"Just since this morning."

"Something's happened to you, Brady. This isn't normal."

"I know."

"Well, do you feel any different?"

"I'm getting a sort of tingling all over, kind of like I stuck my finger in an electrical outlet."

"All the time, or does it come and go?"

"It comes and goes."

"Does it hurt?"

"Not really. I'm kind of getting used to it. You think I should go to the doctor or something? I hate going to the doctor."

"I wouldn't, as long as it doesn't hurt. Maybe you're a genetic mutant, something like that. You get to be fourteen and a half, and this gene nobody else has suddenly kicks in . . ."

"Just what I want to be, a mutant."

"I wish I had it, whatever 'it' is."

With that we got back on our bikes. The easy route home would have been to go through the town of Custer. We stuck to the original plan, hung a hard right, and started the climb up the Needles Highway, another narrow and twisty mountain road. Quinn led the way up, and we didn't do any racing. We stopped at the top where the road threads its way through thirty- and forty-foot granite needles, then we burned down the other side of the mountain through the tunnels and alongside Sylvan Lake, the crown jewel of the Black Hills.

It was late in the afternoon when we rode into Hill City. Both of us found our eyes drawn to Grabba Java. The drive-through was closed, but Maggie was still inside, cleaning up. Crystal was outside at one of the picnic tables, drinking a smoothie.

Naturally we had to stop and check in with her. As we slid in on the other side of the table, Crystal asked about our ride. We said it was great, and then she kind of bit her lip and said, "I hate to tell you this, Brady, but Buzz and Max are really fried at you."

I gulped, and the blood at my temples began to pound. "What about?"

"About that meteorite in your backpack. I made the mistake, I guess, of telling them about it. They told me this long, confusing story about you coming onto their place, them saving you from Attila, you claiming you'd come over to get back a rock that Attila had taken from your mother's flower bed."

"That's all true, except the rock he'd taken from the flower bed was my meteorite."

"That's the part they were fried about, you faking them out, not telling them the truth."

"What exactly did they say?"

"That you were a big liar."

"Nice. I've really done it now. That's the last thing I

need, getting those guys mad at me."

"I'm sorry I brought it up. I thought you'd want to know."

"Don't feel sorry, Crystal. It's all my fault." From the corner of my eye I saw Quinn looking at me like, You didn't tell me about this whole episode, and why not?

Still trying to explain myself to Crystal, I said, "I guess I didn't trust that they'd give it back to me if they knew what it was. You think they would have?"

She would only shrug. "I just hope they let it drop, Brady. Those guys can have long memories."

Tell me about it, I thought.

Crystal said good luck, which was ominous. We got on our bikes and headed for home. We were five minutes down the Mickelson Trail, riding side by side, before I broke the silence. "I'm an idiot," I said.

Quinn didn't want to argue the point. What he said back was "There went our invitation to see those guys demo their catapult."

11

The Meteorite Expert Guy

THE NEXT MORNING WAS Monday, and the museum in Hill City opened at 9:30. We were waiting on the doorstep when it did.

We resisted the temptation to buy any new fossils at the gift shop and headed into the exhibits. Towering above us, Stan the Tyrannosaurus rex was the star attraction. Paleontologists working out of this small but mighty museum had dug up as many T-rexes as the rest of the world combined.

The swinging doors behind the saber-toothed tiger led to the labs and the offices. We were going to need some directions.

Here came a man in a white lab coat with a cup of Grabba Java in his hand. He was moving fast and was headed where we wanted to go. Quinn spoke up, almost stepping into his path. "Excuse me. We're looking for the meteorite expert guy."

I always want scientists to look like Einstein. This one didn't look a bit like Einstein, but he did look eccentric. He was tall as a tree, his face was narrow as a brick, and he had a forest of white ear hair. The scientist stopped and bent down his head like a curious giraffe. "The meteorite expert guy," he repeated thoughtfully, with a very British accent.

"I think he's here just for the summer," I added helpfully.

"My, yes, a fellow by the name of Dr. Ripley Ripley. Can you imagine parents doing that to a child? Let me give you a tip—he doesn't like his first name. He likes his last name just fine."

"Should we call him Dr. Ripley?" I ventured.

"Call me Dr. Rip," he replied with a grin.

We shook hands, told him who we were and where we were from. "I'm from Oxford," he told us, "known for shirts, shoes, and scholars. Now, how may I help you lads?"

I slung off my backpack. "We brought a meteorite for you to look at, Dr. Rip."

"Ah, so you think you've found a meteorite, do you? After our meteor shower, I suppose I'll be looking at quite a few rocks these next few days."

"We're pretty sure this one's the real deal," Quinn said.

Pretty sure? I thought.

67

"The light is much better in my office. Let's go back and have a look, shall we? Follow me back through the warrens, middens, and dolmens, but stay close. You might get lost in geologic time."

Our scientist led us through a big room with a team of dinosaur techies at work. You could see the outlines of the huge fossil bone they were freeing from the surrounding rock with little picks like dental tools. Before long the professor was opening his office door for us.

"Sit down, lads, sit down." We plunked ourselves down on a couch opposite his rolling desk chair, where he was already waiting expectantly.

As I fished in my backpack, the professor reached into the pocket of his lab coat for his glasses. Once they were perched on his nose, he reached out his long arm and took Fred in hand. As he eyeballed the traveler from every angle, the few wisps of hair on the top of his head stood on end. I didn't take that for a reaction, just static electricity due to our dry Black Hills air. The professor wasn't reacting at all.

Quinn shrugged at me. I shrugged back, then ran my eyes over the rocks on the scientist's desk, the computers, the microscopes, a glass cabinet full of vials, star charts on the walls, big enlargements of photos taken by the Hubble Space Telescope.

"It's basaltic, almost certainly," the professor announced at last. "Basaltic shergottite."

My chest tightened up. I had to take a quick breath. "You're saying it's not a meteorite?"

"Beyond question it's a meteorite. Which of you would be the finder?"

"I would be the finder," I volunteered. Quinn looked at me like I was talking funny.

"And what makes you think it was from Saturday evening's event?"

When I explained how I'd come by it, the professor's eyes got big as flying saucers. "Right through your roof and your bed! Bravo! Think of the odds on that!"

"Astronomical," I suggested.

My pun flew past the professor—he was all wound up. "Life is surpassingly strange, my friends, and full of improbable surprises. There's a world of difference between the *improbable* and the *impossible*. Brady's near death by meteorite reminds me of the demise of Aeschylus, one of the great dramatists of ancient Greece, who was killed by a falling tortoise."

"Sick!" Quinn exclaimed. "True story?"

"Indeed. The tortoise, you see, was dropped by a bearded vulture, known for dropping tortoises on rocks in order to crack them open like walnuts. From a height, it has been surmised, the bird mistook the great man's bald head for a rock. Take a certain individual and calculate the odds of him being killed by falling tortoise—oh, my."

Quinn squirmed a little, afraid the professor was going to get us off track. "That's all very interesting, Dr. Rip, but is Brady's meteorite valuable?"

For some reason, the professor didn't seem thrilled

about answering that question. "Relatively speaking, most meteorites are a dime a dozen. Did you know that millions bombard us every year?"

"No way," Quinn objected.

The professor was watching me and saw that I was on his side. He waited to see if I could explain, and I took him up on it. "Most are only as big as a grain of sand, Quinn, or maybe the size of a pebble."

"How come you never told me?"

"I dunno. It never came up."

"Brady's an astronomy freak. Ask him anything, Professor."

"I'd be delighted. Let's start with our own solar system. Name the planets beginning with the one closest to the sun."

I did, adding at the end that Pluto had been disqualified.

"What are the clouds of Venus composed of?"

"Sulfuric acid."

"Can you name the giant moon of Saturn, which has an atmosphere?"

"Titan."

"Bravo. Approximately how many moons has Jupiter?"

"More than sixty."

"Excellent, Brady. Mars has two small moons. Can you name them?"

"Phobos and Deimos. Fear and terror."

"What's unusual about them?"

"Their shape—probably they were asteroids before Mars captured them."

"Brilliant."

I hoped all this quizzing meant the professor was going to tell us some really important stuff, now that he could see I wasn't just some doofus with a meteorite.

"Can you possibly name the largest volcano in the solar system?"

"Olympus Mons, on Mars. Three times higher than Everest."

A smile spread across the professor's face, and those wisps on his dome stood up again. "I have one final question for you, with a bit of a preface. Almost all meteorites come from the asteroid belt, as you no doubt know—from material left over, it's thought, from the beginning of our solar system four and a half billion years ago. Meteorites that don't come from the asteroid belt are younger, much more rare, and of far greater scientific interest. Yours is one of these. Where did it originate?"

I thought and thought. I wracked my brain. "I give up," I said finally.

Quinn jumped up from the couch. "Congratulations, Professor! You finally stumped him. I told you it wouldn't be easy."

Dr. Rip held out the space traveler in his open hand. "Keep in mind, this is a piece of extraterrestrial basalt, which began as molten lava flowing from the gut of a volcano."

"Fred's from Mars?"

"Fred?" wondered the professor. "You've given the meteorite a name?"

"Wait a second," Quinn cried. "Fred can't be from Mars!"

The professor was all intense and aglow. He turned his attention to Quinn. "Consider this, my doubtful friend. Basaltic shergottites on Earth occur *only* in meteorites. As you know, we've been landing Rovers on Mars for decades. The chemical signature of certain rocks on Mars matches perfectly with that of the basaltic shergottites found in the meteorites on Earth."

Quinn was sticking to his guns. "Doesn't make sense. And here's why not: Mars has *gravity*! Rocks don't go flying off the surface of Mars!"

Dr. Rip did a knee slap, and his eyes lit up. "Brilliant objection, but I think you'll enjoy the explanation of how they could do just that. Picture a gigantic asteroid or comet colliding with Mars. Think of the force, and remember this: 'For every action, there's an equal and opposite reaction.' Fred and thousands of his relatives are ejected beyond the gravity of Mars and into their own orbit around the sun. Around and around Fred goes, for millions of years, until one day he is snagged by the gravity of Earth, and down he comes!"

"That's rad," Quinn raved. "Fred got kicked off Mars by a big asteroid! So, let's cut to the chase, Professor. Is he valuable?"

"Quite."

"*How* valuable?"

"Let me put it this way. Only thirty-four Mars rocks have ever been found on Earth."

"Thirty-four! Fred's *extremely* rare, Brady! Take a guess, Professor. How much could Brady get for him?"

Get for him? I thought. Since when had I decided to part company with him?

"I suppose it would depend on whether he sold Fred intact or in slices," the professor replied. "That's not my field, lads. Personally, I find it disturbing whenever they are sold. It's especially a shame when they get diced up and scattered all over."

"Man, oh man," I said. "Have we got a lot to think about. You've been great, Dr. Rip, just great. Thanks!"

The professor turned Fred over in his palm. "Do me one favor. See this nice nub here on his backside? Would you give me this much, let me keep and study this nub off Fred's bottom? For my research? It shouldn't hurt him a bit."

"I guess it's okay," I said, and Quinn nodded his approval.

Dr. Ripley reached for a pair of goggles and disappeared for a few minutes. When he returned with Fred, there was a sawed-off spot where his nub had been. The professor made a small speech. It was the first time he'd ever had a Martian meteorite walk off the street and into his life. "I'm terribly honored and grateful," he told us.

A few minutes later we jumped on our bikes with an appointment to come back at four the next afternoon and find out if the professor had learned anything. We were so pumped up, it felt like our wheels weren't touching the ground.

12

We're Never Going to Forget This

FROM THE MUSEUM WE headed straight home and started shooting baskets. I had so much on my mind, I wasn't very accurate. After I clanged three in a row off the rim, Quinn said, "Hey, Brady, you still feeling that electricity or whatever it is?"

"Some of the time, not all of the time."

"You know what, I wanna see if you can dunk."

"Get out of here, Quinn. That's impossible."

"I'm not kidding. The way you vaulted over that buffalo yesterday, I wouldn't put it past you."

"The buffalo was about to kill me. That was adrenaline."

Quinn flipped me the ball. "What's to lose? Give it your best shot, Brady. Whatever you had yesterday, maybe you've still got it."

He had me wondering. Truth was, I was buzzing like I had my finger in a light socket. To actually jam in front of Quinn would totally blow his mind. His head would go flying off of his shoulders.

I went to the corner of the concrete apron, dribbled a few times, then started toward the basket. Like an NBA star at the slam-dunk contest before the all-star game, I accelerated as I went. Off that last step, I got major air.

Major, major air.

It was beyond beautiful. *What a rush!* I slammed it down with a vengeance.

"That was sick!" Quinn cried. "Do it again!"

And I did, again and again and again, each time differently. "Stuff it!" Quinn kept yelling. "Stuff it, Brady!"

"Enough," I said finally, my heart pounding like thunder. "That was crazy."

"That was insane! You're five-foot-six!"

"There's a five-six guy in the NBA who dunks."

"You're fourteen and he's got muscles! I'm tellin' you, you're a mutant."

"Hey, knock it off, Quinn."

"We have to start thinking about your high school career, Brady. When do you unveil your dunk?"

"They'll think I'm on steroids, and not the kind in my inhaler."

"Let 'em test you! They won't find anything!"

"We're keeping this under wraps, Quinn. You gotta promise me you're not telling anybody, and I mean *anybody*, even your dad. It's way too strange."

Quinn wasn't too keen on it, but I made him promise. I knew I could count on him. We've always kept each other's secrets.

"So, what are we going to do next, Brady? It's still morning and we've got worlds to conquer!"

"Got any ideas?"

"How about the Halls of the Dead—I've been wanting to explore it."

The Halls of the Dead was the name Quinn had given to the cave we'd discovered the summer before. I'd been hoping he wasn't going to bring this up. It had been skin-crawling spooky, and we hadn't even gotten that far in.

"Maybe later," I said. "We could climb Harney . . ."

Mount Harney is only four miles from my house. It's the highest peak east of the Rocky Mountains and is sacred to the Sioux. Every spring, more and more of the Lakota Sioux were coming back to the Black Hills and climbing the mountain for a ceremony they call Welcoming Back the Thunders.

"No sale," Quinn said. "We've been up there a bunch of times."

"What about fishing? I've never seen you turn that down."

"Maybe, if it's something we haven't tried before."

"We haven't ever caught lake trout at Pactola."

"We've tried, from the shore. We don't have a boat, remember?"

"I know where we can get one," I countered, thinking

as fast as I could. "At the Wal-Mart in Custer, they've got a little inflatable raft with oars. With one of those we could get out in the middle of Pactola and troll the deep water."

One thing about Quinn, he's decisive. "Sounds pretty extreme—you talked me into it. We'll get licenses and a couple of new lures. Think the boat is small enough to carry on our bikes?"

"If we take it out of the box, I'm pretty sure it'll fit in one of our backpacks."

"Okay, we head for Custer and buy what we need for the lake. Where's Fred?"

"Still in my backpack."

"That's what I thought. Do you think it's okay to be carting Fred around wherever you go? Is he safe in your backpack? We sure don't want to lose him, not after the professor said he's 'quite' valuable."

"Where else would we put him? I don't want to let him out of my sight. Of course he's safe in my backpack. Who'd take better care of him than me?"

Quinn looked unsure. "What about the Carvers? Remember what Crystal said, how mad they are at you?"

I had to give that some thought. "They might try to trick me, something like that, but they wouldn't just steal him. That's not their style. I'll be super careful."

"Okay, enough jawing. Let's get on the road before we fossilize. If we're quick at the Wal-Mart, we might even make it to Pactola tonight. Fish the lake in the morning and see the professor on the way home."

The town of Custer is ten miles south of home. Halfway there, we stopped for bison burgers at the Crazy Horse Memorial. We ate outdoors in front of the Indian Museum of North America. We had an amazing view of the mountain. Quinn said he could tell that a lot more rock had been removed in the year since he'd seen it.

My dad had taken us up top a few times. Once, we got to stand thirty feet out in front of Crazy Horse's face. It filled up the sky. It was an amazing sight, an amazing feeling. The last time we were up there, we ran way out on his arm.

One of those tiny humans up there drilling on the cliffs at this very moment was a big man named Charlie Steele. I squinted and tried to make my father out. I thought I had him spotted but couldn't be sure.

At first, to hear my dad tell it, Crazy Horse had just been a job, one with more future than gold mining in Lead. As time went by, though, he became as dedicated as the Ziolkowski family, if that's possible.

It all started when Korczak Ziolkowski, an assistant sculptor at Mount Rushmore, got a letter from a Lakota chief named Henry Standing Bear. The chief had been watching the carving of the presidents' faces. He told Korczak that the Indians had great heroes, too. Would Korczak carve a monument to one of their great leaders?

The hero they picked wasn't one remembered for great speeches at signing ceremonies. They chose Crazy Horse, sometimes called Strange Man of the Lakotas, for his powerful and mysterious ways. When he was about my age, he had a vision. He saw himself charging into battle on a spirit horse. The bullets were whistling all around him, but they could never touch him. And they never did.

Bit by bit, the mountain is turning into Crazy Horse the warrior, at the front of every fight, symbol of courage, nobility, and resistance. Crazy Horse was one of the leaders at the Battle of the Little Bighorn when George Armstrong Custer and his men got famously rubbed out in 1876.

Korczak went to work in 1948. For years, he did all the drilling, blasting, and mucking alone. An insane amount of granite had to be removed before he could begin on the actual statue. At the museum you can see old films of him at work on the mountain. As his sons grew up, they joined him. Korczak didn't live long enough to see even the face completed, but his family carries on. More than a million people visit every year, and they donate enough money to keep the dream alive.

When it's finally done, the statue of the Lakota chief on his warhorse will be way bigger than Rushmore. It'll be as long as a cruise ship and tall as a sixty-story skyscraper.

Crazy Horse will be pointing into the distance. The gesture comes from a moment in history. A year after the Battle of the Little Bighorn, Crazy Horse's band was on the verge of starvation. The last herds of buffalo had been killed so the Indians wouldn't have anything to eat.

Crazy Horse came to a fort to listen to promises about food and blankets. When he did, he was taunted by an Army officer: "So where are your lands now, Crazy Horse?"

Crazy Horse pointed to the horizon and said, "My lands are where my dead lie buried."

As soon as Crazy Horse saw they were going to put him in jail, he resisted. He was held from behind, and they ran him through with a bayonet. Crazy Horse was still young, only a couple of years over thirty.

Quinn knows all the history. We didn't talk about it over burgers, about the Carvers either, though we both might have been thinking about them, too. I know I was.

It was all because of my dad working at Crazy Horse, and me feeling the same way he did, that Max and Buzz had a grudge against me. They'd been carrying it since fourth grade, when we studied the Black Hills in social studies practically all year.

Along about April, I gave my big report on the history of the Crazy Horse Memorial. I laid it on thick about George Armstrong Custer, how he was no hero like he used to be considered. This wasn't really news, even in the Black Hills.

The next kid up was Max Carver. He stood up in front of the class, glared at me, then announced the topic of his report. It was about an ancestor on his mother's side, a cavalry officer who rode and died with Custer. Uh-oh.

How was I to know? Every kid in class, even the

teacher, turned and looked at me. They knew I was in for it.

I never got beat up or anything like that. Maybe if I had, it would have been over with. Like Max told me after school, "We're never going to forget this, Steele."

And they never had.

13

Discount Shopping

WE PULLED INTO CUSTER and headed for the Wal-
Mart. It didn't take long to find the little inflatable raft I'd told Quinn about. The *Challenger* was made
in China, ours for only $39.99. Its plastic oars came in
two pieces that you screwed together, and they would
pack nicely. We began to wonder, though, about our fishing rods back home. They didn't break down small
enough to carry on our bikes.

A couple of aisles over we found telescoping fishing
poles for $19.99, also from China, that came with reel
and line. You could carry one in your back pocket. It was
the name that closed the deal; it was called the
Eliminator. My eighth-grade English teacher would have
gotten a kick out if that. He was always preaching
against "thesaurus abuse."

We threw two Eliminators into the cart and picked out some new lures. Lake trout are known to favor big, shiny spoons. It takes something flashy to lure them out of the depths.

As we stood at the counter waiting to buy our fishing licenses, we got to figuring how much storage we'd have left after filling one backpack with the raft. Basically, we had the other backpack and our bike panniers, which we always called our saddlebags. "I can tell you right now," Quinn said, "there's no way we're going to have room for your tent."

"Good point," I had to admit.

We found the solution across from where we were standing: an item by the uninspired name of Tube Tent, ours for $3.99. It weighed next to nothing and wouldn't take up any space.

Our shopping expedition had been the way we like it—quick. We got on the Mickelson Trail and blasted home to start packing.

Half a mile short of our driveway, we crossed the Carvers' driveway. Attila had stationed himself there as if waiting for somebody to come home. I'd never seen him do that before.

Here was something else I'd never seen. Attila started following us. Following me, to be exact, hanging right by my side.

The most surprising part was, it wasn't like he wanted a piece of me. The way he kept looking at me as he ran alongside, it was more like we were old buddies.

"What's that about?" Quinn called.

"No idea," I replied. At first I tried yelling, "Go home, Attila, go home!" as I kept riding. He kept bounding alongside, unfazed. I put on a burst of speed, thinking I'd leave him in the dust, but he took it for a game and left *me* in the dust. I'd never seen a dog run that fast in my life. A greyhound would have choked on his exhaust.

"Will you look at that," Quinn marveled. "That beats everything."

The war dog was waiting for us at my driveway. Strangely, his tongue wasn't even hanging out. I yelled at him to go home, this time at the top of my lungs. He barked back at me, at the top of *his* lungs, then wagged his tail. Not only that, he began to whine, like I'd hurt his feelings.

We rode on up to the house, Attila trotting alongside. "Call the Carvers?" Quinn wondered.

Before I even had to face the thought, Attila bounded for home across the footbridge and over the barbed wire fence. We shrugged, headed inside, and started pulling out our camping equipment.

It was killing me to leave so much stuff behind, like cooking gear, my little Primus stove, and especially food. According to Quinn, all we needed was two plastic bowls and two plastic spoons, some granola, and some powdered milk. "It's just an overnight," Quinn said. "We're not gonna starve."

I had to admit, he had a point. By the time we got

through packing our sleeping bags, fishing gear, jackets and rain gear, and so on, there wasn't room for our toothbrushes.

"It's almost 3:30," I said. "You still think we can make it to the lake before dark?"

"Sure, but we better get going."

I wrote my dad a note, told him where we were headed, said we'd be back tomorrow. He'd always been fine about me going off camping with Quinn, no problem.

Within a half hour we were blazing north through Hill City. No time to stop in and see Crystal. She spotted us flying by, though, and gave us a wave.

From home it was a twenty-mile ride to the lake. Days were long, but we were going to have to blister some asphalt to beat the dark. As soon as we left Spring Creek, we started climbing the first grade. The clouds were building, and the wind was blowing against us. On the merits of my riding the day before, Quinn had me out front, drafting him. With all the weight we were pushing, this should have been a killer, but it wasn't. Strange as it still seemed, I was going to have to watch my speed so I didn't run Quinn into the ground.

Traffic was heavy, including hordes of bikers southbound out of Deadwood. What a roar they made. No helmets on any of them, I noticed: like Uncle Jake, they were more afraid of helmet hair than they were of death.

The wind was blowing harder all the time, always against us. Slow and steady, we won the race. The sun was about to crash into a mountain as we pulled into the campground at Pactola Lake.

The place was jam-packed. Every corner we turned, we found kids running around, music playing, dogs barking, steaks sizzling on the grills, picnic tables filling with food. Our chances of finding a campsite appeared to be south of zero.

We downshifted past a couple of girls who checked us out with mild interest. No doubt they were thinking of inviting us to dinner. Hey, guys, we have tons of food. We'll tell Dad to throw on a couple more steaks. Look, here's a spot where you can pitch your tent right next to our RV. After dinner we can go for a long walk around the lake.

Yeah, right. Truth be told, they were like bored trout watching a couple of fishermen go by in a drift boat. "They had no idea they should be asking for your T-shirt," Quinn said with a sly grin.

On we went, hopes dimming. Just when we thought we'd have to crash in the woods somewhere, we found the last untaken campsite. It had a latrine view and a bit of a latrine smell, but otherwise it was perfect. We decided not to bother pitching the tube tent. We'd use it for a ground cloth, throw our sleeping bags on it, and sleep under the stars.

Quinn got out the bowls and spoons, mixed up some powdered milk, and set out our ration of granola. He said it was excellent, but he was lying. "Let's play some cards. Bet you brought 'em."

"Yeah, and a flashlight. It's getting dark."

I fetched my backpack and started pulling things out, including my fleece jacket. The night air was suddenly cold. Something fell out of my balled-up jacket and hit the ground with a thud. It was Fred.

Just then a guy drove by selling firewood out of his truck. Quinn bought a couple armfuls. We were able to start our card game by the light of a toasty campfire. We stayed up late, as late as the last barking dog in the campground.

14

The Worm Grunter

THE FIRST RUMBLE CAME about 1:30 in the morning. The thunder sounded far off but ominous. I wondered if Quinn heard it, but I wasn't going to ask. Ten minutes later, the lightning strobes were making it easy for me to look at my watch and time the thunder. The storm was about eight miles away. I got up on one elbow. "Hear that, Quinn?"

"Fuhgeddaboudit, it'll go away," he mumbled.

I tried to fuhgeddaboudit. Five minutes later, here came thunder strong enough to loosen our fillings, and the wind started blowing hard. "Tube tent," Quinn announced, and we sprang into action.

I grabbed the parachute cord we'd brought along and fed it through the tubular sheet of flimsy orange plastic we'd thrown down and gone to sleep on. We ran in opposite directions for trees to tie to, just like in the picture that came with the tube tent.

The so-called tent was shown with a perfectly triangular opening at each end. At the moment, ours looked like a housepainter's drop cloth flapping on a clothesline. We found a few rocks and threw them inside to try to spread the thing out and make a floor.

Our shelter without poles and doors was as pitched as we were going to get it. We dove inside with our sleeping bags just as the storm broke. Wouldn't you know it was a smackdown gullywasher. Thirty seconds was all it took before a stream deep enough to float trout was rushing through our little home in the woods. The rain lashed our faces as we held up the floor at the uphill entrance, trying to keep the flood out.

"Get under the picnic table?" I suggested. My question was answered by the next bolt of lightning, which revealed a pond collecting under the table.

"Run for the outhouse?" wondered Quinn.

"No sale," I replied.

Fifteen minutes, and the cloudburst had swept on through. "That was fairly extreme," I said.

"Insane," Quinn agreed.

We put on our jackets and thrashed around in our wet bags trying to get back to sleep. Quinn's teeth were chattering, but mine weren't. He asked if I wasn't freezing. "Not too bad," I said. The weird thing was, I wasn't cold at all.

Next thing I knew, Quinn was shaking me awake.

Morning had come, but the sun hadn't reached our campsite yet. Quinn hadn't slept at all and was on fire to go fishing. He'd already fixed our granola by the time I dragged myself to the picnic table.

Catching a truly big fish had always been one of our major goals in life, and lake trout are big. The Pactola Lake record was twenty-five pounds. We'd tried casting from the shore a couple of times over the years, caught some rainbows and German browns but never a lake trout. As everybody knows, you have to fish *deep* for lake trout, deeper and deeper as the summer goes along. They like to hang out down where the water is coldest. With a boat, we could get out on the lake and fish the deep water.

After chowing down on granola, we threw our tent in the trash and bicycled down to the lake. I started pumping up the *Challenger* with its little plastic pump. The ribs of the inflatable floor took shape nicely. Slowly but surely, the perimeter tube began to rise. While I pumped, Quinn assembled the two-piece oars and fooled with our fishing gear. The lake was mirror-calm and the sun was shining bright.

Our raft looked awful small as we walked it out to knee-deep water, but we weren't talking about it. Quinn got in first. I handed him the Eliminators, then slipped the oars through the plastic oarlocks and climbed aboard carefully. The outside tube wasn't really substantial enough to sit on—the lake would have poured in. As pictured on the box, we sat on the floor facing each other, my legs inside Quinn's. My backpack, with tackle and Fred inside, sat between us. We might've looked silly, like two men in a tub, but nobody was watching and we were crazed with fish lust, which is indescribable if you aren't a fisherman. It consumes you utterly, turns you into a prehistoric, spear-chucking caveman.

Quinn hung on to the Eliminators as I rowed in the direction of the island that always appears on the Pactola postcards. It was still so early, there wasn't a motorboat on the lake, but there would be anytime now. We were feeling lucky. Fishing tends to be best early, especially on sunny days.

The going was slow because the oars and the oar-locks were so rinky. Finally we reached water deep enough to start fishing. Quinn was sure he had the hot ticket, a huge silver spoon with revolving red eyes. I selected a giant red and white Daredevil.

We soon discovered we had a problem. We needed to keep the boat moving, but with those toy oars, we couldn't get up enough speed to give the lures trailing behind us any action. We were getting some curious looks from the suddenly plentiful motorboats. After an hour with me working those oars fast as eggbeaters and still no bites, we headed for shore in utter defeat. "The *Challenger* was challenging, all right," Quinn said sourly.

"It isn't built for speed, I'll give you that."

"What's it built for, Brady?"

"Swimming pool."

The closest shoreline was a campsite where an old guy with a grizzled beard was sitting on a lawn chair in front of his camper and watching us come in. He wasn't laughing, which was good. Fishing can make you feel murderous at times, especially when people are watching you make a fool of yourself.

We staggered ashore. The old guy looked sympathetic. He asked if we wanted some fried chicken.

"Fried chicken?" Quinn echoed. "We accept!"

The old guy went into his camper and came back with enough fried chicken and potato salad to choke an army, along with sodas, pickles, and chips. Life was good again.

"Call me Curly," our benefactor told us. We got the joke—his head was slick as a billiard ball. Curly told us he was from Missouri, and that he hadn't shaved since he left home in June. We told him we'd been trying to troll for lake trout.

"Forget the lures, boys. I suggest you try worms. You won't have to troll. Just sit out there and wait for them to bite."

When we mentioned we didn't have any worms, Curly replied, "No problem. I'm an old worm grunter."

Worm grunter? That was a new one on us. As we got into the pickles and chips, the old-timer produced a heavy wooden stake, a sledgehammer, a pair of gloves, and a serious strap of metal, which he called a stob. Curly put his gloves on, pounded the stake into the ground, and began to rub the stob back and forth over the top of the stake, faster and faster. He was sure enough grunting all the while.

Pretty soon Curly was so red in the face I thought I was going to see my first heart attack. What we saw instead, all around us, were worms coming up out of the ground—huge night crawlers. "Grab 'em, boys, grab 'em! Soon as I quit, they'll dive back under!"

We collected two dozen or so crawlers fast enough to avert Curly's coronary, then put them in a paper box we had emptied of fried chicken. "Fish the lake bottom," the old guy wheezed. "I hear it's a hundred and fifty feet deep—that's where the lake trout will be."

We had to admit we didn't have any bait holder hooks or weights to get our lines down to the bottom.

"Got plenty," Curly said. In no time at all he had us totally rigged up. He even packed our crawlers with wet moss. We thanked him and climbed back into the *Challenger*.

15

You Guys Got a Problem

QUINN HAD A TAKE-NO-PRISONERS set to his jaw as I rowed us around and beyond the island. "We're going for deep water," my cousin declared. "I mean, *deep* water, where monsters dwell."

"Extreme fishing," I chanted. "This is gonna be epic. Today we bust a blue whale."

We'd soon be out among the motorboats, but we weren't worried about getting sunk and dismembered—they were fishing. They'd killed their big outboard motors and switched to their little electric trolling motors. Two or three miles an hour was all they were going.

The only boat roaring around on the lake was one pulling a water-skier, a mile away at least. Pactola is nearly three miles long, and they had plenty of water to play with. A lot of days you won't see anybody waterskiing on Pactola. It can get windy and the water is way cold. The Carver boys sometimes skied it, though. I was hoping this wasn't them.

Quinn was on the same wavelength as he squinted into the distance. "That better not be the *Corpse Hunter*."

"If it is," I said, "they'll never know we're out here."

That name we'd made up for their boat—*Corpse Hunter*—was a closely held secret. You didn't kid Buzz and Max about their father being the coroner. Not that they didn't sometimes talk about the "stiffs," as they liked to call them. You got the idea they'd seen more than a few. They'd even shown us the hook that their daddy drags behind the family motorboat to snag corpses off the bottom of the lake.

"No worries," I declared. "What are the chances that's them? They're home finishing their catapult."

I quit rowing. It was time to deploy Curly's night crawlers. I chose two of the juiciest and baited the hooks. We lowered away, Quinn off of one side, me off the other.

It took a good while for our weights to hit bottom, and then we waited. We remembered to loosen the drag on our reels. The line was only 8-lb. test. A big lake trout would snap the line in a hurry if it couldn't run with it.

The wind came up a little, but we were still comfortable in our T-shirts. A fisherman on a boat a hundred yards away was hooked up with a rod-bending fish. It had to be a lake trout. The battle went on for a good ten minutes before one of his buddies netted the lunker and brought it over the side. The sound of their celebrating made us feel empty and rotten. We were suffering some serious fish envy.

"They caught it trolling with a big old spoon," Quinn said darkly.

"We trust in worms," I maintained. "You know what, Quinn? We didn't bring a net. How are we gonna get a big one into the boat?"

"If we get a fish on, maybe we can holler to one of the other boats and they'll loan us theirs."

"Good plan."

That plan had no future. Here came the boat pulling the water-skier, down toward our end of the lake. There went all the boats that were fishing, toward the water the ski boat had vacated.

Before long we were hit by the wake from the speeding boat. The first wave had come from a distance and wasn't all that powerful, but even so it splashed over the side of our raft. We motioned for them to back off.

If they'd seen us, they didn't let on. They kept coming. There were two guys inside the boat, a driver and a passenger. The water-skier, a big guy, was skiing slalom, snowboard-style. You had to be good to do that. He was wearing a wet suit and kicking up quite a plume. "That skier has a buzz haircut," I reported.

Quinn took another look, then groaned. "That's Buzz, no question about it. Maybe the *Corpse Hunter* hasn't recognized us. Try not to look at 'em."

"Believe me, I won't."

"Hey, Brady, check out my rod tip!"

My head jerked around. The tip of Quinn's Eliminator was getting some action. He saw it, and I saw it, and neither one of us said another word.

Down went Quinn's rod tip again, but not convincingly. It was just another nibble. Another little piece of the worm had just been bitten off.

For about five seconds, nothing. Quinn and I exchanged glances, wondering if his fish was going to come back for the big chomp. Sometimes they don't.

This one did. When the chomp came, Quinn set the hook like a pro. Then, *ziiiiiiiiiiing*, the line went screaming off his reel. "Fish on!" Quinn cried. "Has to be a lake trout!" Quick as I could, I reeled in my own line so it wouldn't get tangled with his.

That first run nearly took all hundred yards off Quinn's reel. Another few seconds and the 8-lb. test would've snapped. Luckily, the lunker did a U-turn. Quinn reeled furiously enough to keep tension on the line. His spool was half-full again when the trout ripped off another run. Quinn hung on like he was riding a bucking bronco. "This thing's gotta be huge, Brady. A behemoth. Here, fishie, here, fishie."

The battle raged on with run after run. Quinn's Eliminator was bent in an absolute horseshoe. "This is killing me," he cried. "My arms are cramping like crazy."

It was easy to see why. Quinn's biceps and forearms were like rope at the snapping point. The cords in his neck were tight as bowstrings, and his face was seriously purple.

We heard the roar of the Carvers' boat, knew they were getting closer. From the corner of my eye I saw Buzz at the end of the tow rope. The arc he was carving with his slalom ski was going to take him real close to us.

As Buzz raced by, he was strong enough to hang on with only one hand. He waved big as life with the other and yelled, "DON'T HORSE HIM, QUINN!"

A second later we got totally doused by the spray off his ski. Two seconds after that we got rocked by a major wake from their boat that left the *Challenger* half-full of water.

"Thanks a lot!" Quinn yelled, but of course they couldn't hear. Max, riding shotgun in the boat, was pointing back at us and laughing. The driver was big brother Cal—Silent Cal, as Quinn always called him. Cal must have been loving this, too. Speed and intimidation were his game, whether it was running the football and knocking guys down or climbing up their tailpipe behind the wheel of his 1970 Mercury Spoiler.

I splashed water fast as I could out of the raft. "Fish still on?"

Quinn nodded. "No thanks to them."

The Carvers veered off in another direction. We could only hope they were gone for good.

Quinn began to gain on his adversary. At last we saw a flash in the dark green depths. A few minutes later we got a much better look. We saw the laker's giant head, its long, beefy body, even the spots along its sides. "That's no fish," I said, "that's a Jurassic ichthyosaur. We should give him a name."

"You give him a name. I'm busy."

"How about Stan, after the T-rex in the museum?"

"Stan it is. Hey, Brady, we need a plan. Without a net, we've got no chance."

"No boats close now, except for the *Corpse Hunter*. They might have a net. Should I wave 'em over?"

"Do it. Do it now!"

I looked over and saw the Carver boat standing still. Buzz was climbing back in. I waved them over, furiously.

No question about it, our monster was tiring. We got all sorts of good looks as he swam back and forth, sounded, then came back up and thrashed the surface.

Here came the Carvers, in a hurry, but that's what we'd asked them to do. Cal roared close, too close, then cut the power back suddenly. "You guys got a net?" I yelled.

They looked around. "Sorry," Max said with perverse satisfaction. "Usually we do."

"What a whopper," Buzz gushed. "Like I said, Quinn, don't horse him. Whatever you do, don't horse him."

Stan came to the surface again, gave us our best look yet. "That thing'll go over thirty pounds!" Buzz cried. "Pactola record!"

The *Corpse Hunter* drifted closer yet. "Give Quinn some space," I pleaded.

"What's the harm?" snapped Silent Cal, but he knew what I was talking about. When you're trying to land a big fish, the last thing you want is an audience.

I tried to put the Carvers out of my mind. "Try to work him against the raft, Quinn. I'll flip him inside with my hands."

Max laughed. "This I gotta see. Hey, check it out, he's barely hooked."

Three times Quinn got the big one close to my hands, oh, so close. Each time, Stan would summon strength and dive. The fourth time, Quinn guided his whale right alongside the raft. I reached out, but Stan's big old eye saw my grasping hands and he went into a frenzy. The monster beat the water to a froth and twisted away. "Gimme one more chance," I pleaded.

Quinn turned our prize once more, and here it came, once more right along the raft. Now was the time to strike, and I struck. I pinned Stan against the tube and began to work him up and up so I could flip him inside.

Stan was right there, completely out of the water, for a moment that will live forever in infamy. Our dream trout was in my hands, but the hook at the corner of his mouth was gone. Quinn's line was blowing limply in the wind.

I tried my best to hang on, but Stan was so strong and so slippery. With a whip of his spine he slipped free. As bad luck would have it he fell into the lake, not the raft.

A few strokes of his mighty tail and Stan was headed for deep water. There he went, disappearing where the green water meets the black, and then he was gone.

We were too stunned, too sick, to even speak. I glanced over at the *Corpse Hunter* and found them smirking.

"Hey, look at your boat," Buzz yelled. "You guys got a problem."

Buzz was right. The *Challenger* was deflating fast.

"Fish hook must've got it," Quinn said. We were wallowing in water. In a few seconds, the floor of the raft would be our only flotation.

"Looks like you guys could use some help," Buzz observed, and Cal brought the *Corpse Hunter* alongside.

Quinn handed our rods up to Max, who was still smirking. "Hey, nice rods." I'd never felt this humiliated in my entire life. In defeat, in helplessness, I handed my backpack from our sinking raft to Buzz's outstretched hand. I still can't believe what happened next. He fumbled it, just dropped it into the lake.

Fred, I remembered a moment too late. Fred's in that backpack!

Just that fast, I went over the side. I kicked and dove and I followed my backpack down, down, down. It was sinking fast, into murkier and murkier water, but I kept stroking and kicking hard as I could. Strangely, I wasn't feeling the cold or the pressure on my eardrums.

A couple more kicks and I've got it, I thought, but the water was getting almost black. With a last lunge I felt the backpack slip through my fingers. Then it was gone, swallowed up by the pitch dark.

It was a long, long way back up. How had I managed to dive so deep? I wondered how I could've done that, but then I knew. I didn't understand, but I knew.

I exploded through the surface, gasping for air.

"Sorry about the backpack," Buzz said as he hauled me aboard the *Corpse Hunter*. "How weird was that? That thing sank like a rock. Man, I can't believe how long you were down."

"What was in it?" Max asked a little suspiciously.

I had to think fast. "My inhaler," I sputtered.

"I can't believe you aren't breathing any harder, Steele. What about your asthma?"

"I haven't had an attack in, like, a year."

"Sank like a rock," Max repeated suspiciously. "Hmmmm . . ."

16

Extreme Is the Word

OUR RIDE BACK TO Hill City was clouded with gloom. Gloom and disaster and defeat. Thanks to my utter and clueless stupidity, Fred was now on the bottom of the lake. I'd had him only sixty-some hours, not even long enough to look into how much he was worth, and I'd already lost him.

"Quite valuable," I kept hearing the professor say.

"He's safe in my backpack," I heard myself assuring Quinn.

Back at the boat ramp, the Carvers had offered to throw our bikes in the back of their daddy's pickup and drop us at home. This was totally rubbing it in. "No, thanks," I muttered, and we got on our bikes. Out on the highway Cal honked as their pickup roared by towing the *Corpse Hunter*. Max leaned out the window and gave us a gleeful wave.

The Carver boys were soon out of sight. Unfortunately they weren't out of mind. I knew exactly what it was like inside the cab of that truck. We'd given them so much to hoot at and laugh about, it was pathetic.

Quinn had a black cloud over his head, too. I could feel it from my vantage point as I pedaled behind his rear wheel. "I'm leading," he had announced as were leaving Pactola. "Let's get out of here."

Quinn had had it. He was disgusted, and I didn't blame him one bit.

As we pulled into Hill City, neither of us even glanced over at Grabba Java. It felt like we were riding in a dark tunnel. I was surprised when Quinn slowed down and stopped in front of the museum.

I looked at my watch. Four o'clock. We were right on time for our appointment with the professor, but what was the point of going through with it now?

Quinn put his bike in the bike rack and I did the same. He couldn't even look me in the eye. "You know they're going to drag the lake," he muttered.

"I'm afraid so. What are the chances of them hooking my backpack?"

"P.D.G."

P.D.G. was our shorthand for "pretty darn good." This was the last thing I wanted to hear, but Quinn was right. "Probably we won't even find out if they recover him," I said.

"You got that right. They'll slice him and dice him and sell him in tiny pieces on eBay, and you'll never even know. Let's go see the professor, Brady."

"Do we have to?"

"Of course we have to. You have to tell him you lost Fred. Might as well get it over with. Don't you want to find out what he's learned? What happened to your curiosity?"

"Okay, but don't lay it on so thick, Quinn. I feel like a gob of slime as it is."

A minute later our English scientist was ushering us into his office. "Mighty serious this afternoon, are we, lads? I'm happy to see it—this is serious stuff."

Quinn and I settled onto the couch as the tall professor landed in the rolling chair in front of his computer. I was just about to cough it up about losing Fred when the professor declared, "Let's get right to it, then! I'll begin by showing you a photograph."

"Fred through the microscope?" Quinn guessed.

"No, not Fred." Dr. Ripley put his spidery fingers to the keyboard and punched up a grainy black-and-white photograph. It showed a couple of wormlike blobs against a sandy background. "What you're looking at is perhaps the most controversial photograph in all of science. It's from ALH84001, found in 1984 on the Antarctic ice cap but not recognized as a Mars meteorite until 1993. On August 6, 1996, NASA scientists brought it to the attention of the world as compelling evidence of life beyond our planet."

"They look kind of like fishing worms," I said.

"They do, don't they? But keep in mind, this photograph was taken through an electron microscope. The magnification is more than ten thousand times greater than you can achieve with a microscope that uses light. What those NASA scientists thought they were looking at were colonies of bacteria. If confirmed, their discovery would have constituted a monumental milestone in human knowledge. The confirmation, however, never came. The skeptics, and there were many, maintained that these structures might *resemble* bacterial colonies, but resemblance was hardly scientific evidence. Ever since, we've all been waiting for a definitive breakthrough—for superior evidence, or better yet, actual proof that life exists beyond the planet Earth."

"If those were supposed to be colonies," I said, "the bacteria themselves have got to be tiny beyond belief."

"Indeed. You have trillions like them that help out in your digestive system, Brady, trillions of tiny, tiny living creatures that are not human. Fewer than five percent of the species that live in our guts have even been identified!"

"That's pretty extreme," Quinn said, "living in stomach acid and all that."

Those wisps of white hair on top of the professor's shiny head were waving back and forth like cobras above a snake charmer's basket. "*Extreme* is the word, Quinn! Of all the extremophiles—life-forms that thrive in extreme environments—the vast majority are bacteria.

You'll find them feeding on poisonous chemicals around vents on the deep-sea floor; you'll find them at home in boiling pools in Yellowstone National Park; you'll even find them a mile below the surface of the Earth digesting basalt rock!"

"That last kind I've never heard about," I said. "Can bacteria live in solid rock, Dr. Rip?"

"Absolutely! That's what the study of geobiology is all about—life in rock! This photograph you're looking at, and the scientific paper published with it, practically created exobiology, also called astrobiology or space biology, the study of life beyond our planet. The search is on, with Mars being the most likely place to look. We've landed more Rovers, but they've barely scratched the surface, and only in a few spots."

"So, what about Fred?" Quinn reminded the professor. "What have you found out?"

"Ah, what about Fred, indeed. Step up, lads, and take a look into the electron microscope. You first, Brady, Fred's your baby."

Now wasn't the right time to tell the professor, that was for sure. I peered into the microscope and saw five objects shaped like tubes, like worms. "They're wiggling," I reported.

I looked away from the microscope, to the professor. He was so beside himself, I thought he was going to explode.

Quinn came to the microscope and took a good, long look. "You're telling us these are actual Martians?"

"By the many thousands, from that nub off Fred's bottom."

"That's impossible!"

The professor was on his feet and dancing some kind of a jig. "Why, Quinn, why is that impossible?"

"You told us yourself. Fred has been flying around in space for millions of years. Even if the bacteria were eating on Fred when he was still on his home planet, how could they possibly have survived for millions of years in space?"

"*Because they're extremophiles!* Life is surpassingly strange, my friends, and wonderful beyond imagining. All that time these microbes were dormant, and now they've come back to life!"

"Dormant for millions of years and they've come back to life? Has anything on Earth ever done that?"

"Absolutely, and I'll give you an example. Bacteria from the Permian Age, over two hundred million years old, dehydrated and dormant in a New Mexico salt bed, came out of their dormancy and caused the decay of fish that had been packed with the salt!"

Quinn nodded approvingly. "That's insane, Dr. Rip. So what exactly did you do with Fred's nub?"

"To begin with, I ground his nub into a fine powder. I tried water and a nutrient at first—table sugar—with no result. I conjectured that water in its pure and ordinary form might be drowning the little Martians, so I tried again with spit and no sugar, solely my own saliva. I guessed it might prove conducive, and it worked! They came to life! What you see through that microscope is nothing less than the Holy Grail of astrobiology—proof positive of life beyond the planet Earth. This might even mean the Nobel Prize!"

Suddenly, Quinn was looking at me strangely. I had to stop and think what that was all about. It wasn't a look that meant, Go ahead and tell him that Fred's on the bottom of the lake. It was a look that said, I know what's gotten into you and where it came from.

"One caution," the professor said. "Some of us astro-biologists, myself included, have theorized that the history of life on Earth has occasionally had its course altered by the arrival of dormant microbes from space. The ones that fell on fertile soil, so to speak, sprang to life and survived. We have no way of knowing what species may never have existed, including ourselves, without extraterrestrial influence."

"That's an extreme idea," marveled Quinn. "But why is that anything to worry about?"

"Extinctions of species! The history of first contact with exotic microorganisms can be rather frightening. Consider the host of diseases that the Europeans brought to the New World, smallpox being the deadliest. On the heels of the Spanish conquest, millions upon millions of people died, up to ninety percent of the population of Mesoamerica. It may have been the greatest die-off in human history. The native people had no immunities against germs their bodies had never fought before. This is why the astronauts returning from the first moon landing were quarantined for a period of time, to ensure they didn't come down sick from exposure to extraterrestrial microbes."

"Amazing," I said.

"Theoretically, a disease brought from the moon could have spread through the entire human race."

"In that case," Quinn said with a grin, "how come you've been studying Fred here in your office, instead of some high-tech containment lab? I mean, were you even wearing a mask?"

"You've got a point," Dr. Ripley replied. "Here's why I wasn't concerned. After the moon landings, the world's scientific community learned that moon rocks and Mars rocks occur naturally on Earth, having been ejected from the moon and from Mars by asteroid impacts and such. We all set aside our fears of extraterrestrial disease. Those thirty-four Mars rocks I've told you about, shaved into many pieces in some cases, have been handled endlessly in labs and gem shows. Nothing's ever happened."

"Bet you anything," Quinn said with a glance in my direction, "Fred's bugs turn out to be the good kind, like the ones in our guts that help us digest food. They might, like, affect our muscles and make them stronger."

"Wouldn't that be marvelous," the professor agreed.

A few minutes later we were back at the bike rack in front of the museum. "I admit it," I said before Quinn could beat me to the punch. "I was too chicken to bring up losing Fred."

"Good thing. The news might've killed the professor. No meteorite, no Nobel Prize. Tell him sometime later. Here's what I want to know—did you ever spit on Fred?"

"I don't think so . . . Let me think. Oh yeah, sort of."

"What do you mean, 'sort of'?"

"That morning you got here, I woke up with Fred against the side of my face, at the corner of my mouth. I was drooling all over him, actually."

"Well, that explains it. Not only did you drool on Fred and activate the microbes, you even got the microbes in your mouth. Makes me wish I'd chewed on Fred instead of only handling him. Now we have to hope the Carvers don't drag him up and catch his bugs."

"That doesn't sound very likely."

"Can you imagine what they'd be like on the football field all juiced with bacterial Martians? How many guys would they kill in their first game?"

17

Boldness or Folly?

IT WAS NEARLY SIX by the time we reached home, and I was expecting my dad to be back from work. His pickup wasn't around, but Uncle Jake's Harley was parked out front. We went inside to see what that was all about.

We found a note. The two of them had taken off for western Wyoming. They'd gone over there so my father could check out the area around the Jonah gas field where Uncle Jake was looking at working. I asked Quinn where exactly that was. "Fifty miles past nowhere" was all he would say.

The note said they'd be away for two nights, possibly three if Uncle Jake decided to go ahead and move the household stuff from Lead to the trailer he'd rented on the July trip with Quinn. My dad said he thought the two of us could fend for ourselves for a few days.

I got a large pizza out of the freezer and heated it up. Quinn noticed an empty to-go cup from Grabba Java. He wondered if his dad had mustered the courage to go back to Maggie's window. It came out kind of sour instead of as a joke. His mind was on Wyoming, on leaving the Black Hills. He'd just found out it was almost a sure thing, and he was sick about it. I knew he didn't want to talk about it, not now.

As we were devouring the pizza, I asked Quinn if he wanted to play some one-on-one. "Nah," he said. "Maybe another time."

It wasn't like he meant anything by it, but this hurt. Quinn was *always* up for shooting hoops, and he was at his best when he was taking out his frustration about something or other.

Duh, I realized, no wonder he doesn't want to play. He was picturing me running circles around him and dunking. I could try to make a joke and say I'd go easy on him. Right now, he wouldn't think that was very funny.

I got up and put away the plates. "Another time, sure," I said from the sink. "It's been a long day. What are you up for?"

"Video games, I guess. Maybe some TV."

We played *Snowboarding for the Insane*, then *Skateboarding for the Insane*. He'd given them to me, one for Christmas and the other for my birthday. With Quinn's lightning-fast reflexes, he'd always had the edge when it came to video games, and that's the way it went for an hour or so, with him winning most games but not by much.

The only thing was, it wasn't like old times. He was agitated from the start. "You're doggin' it," he said finally. "You're faster than that."

"No way," I protested. "I'm giving it my best shot."

Truth was, I *wasn't* giving it my best shot. Talk about reflexes: mine were so hair-triggered, I could have slaughtered him. I was buzzing like a live wire. I felt like I could've beat the world's fastest human out of the starting blocks in the hundred meters.

Quinn got up and went to the couch. "Let's see what's on TV."

My cousin started surfing channels and landed on a cable program about extreme adventures called *Boldness or Folly?* It was going to feature three different maniacs—a guy trying to row a small boat from California to China, a guy trying to swim 3,400 miles down the Amazon, and a woman trying to make it to both Poles, on foot, alone. Quinn couldn't believe it when I told him I was too wasted to stay up.

I dragged myself upstairs and sat on the edge of my bed. Quinn might wish he had whatever bug I had, but I was already hoping it would run its course and soon. All I wanted to be was normal, and have things with Quinn back the way they used to be. As far as I was concerned, Quinn would always be top dog, but how was that going to work if I could drop him on every climb, stuff the basketball in his face, and annihilate him every time we played a video game?

I got into bed and crashed. I crashed hard, into a bizarre series of dreams. At first I was diving, endlessly diving, for my sinking backpack. I swam all the way to the bottom of the lake. Somehow I was able to see a few feet ahead in the murk. I swam every which way in search of my backpack but kept getting faked out by rocks that looked like backpacks.

Stan swam by, and he gave me the evil eye. I knew it was him because he was as big as a king salmon and the side of his mouth was torn. I reached out and tried to touch him, but he swam away. I've been down too long, I thought. My brains are about to blow out through my ears. I panicked and went up too fast, my head began to explode, and then I was at a football game.

Hill City was playing Custer under the lights. Our Rangers were stomping the Wildcats thanks to Max and Buzz. Both weighed over three hundred pounds, somebody was saying. I was in high school, I realized. Crystal was sitting next to me in the stands. I had the feeling she was my girlfriend, but I wasn't sure. Maybe not. After the game was over, we went our separate ways.

I was taking a shortcut to get to my car. Out of nowhere, who but the Carver boys appeared, all three, still in pads. They cornered me against a fence, tackled me, then sat on me. I felt like a snail getting crushed out of its shell. Max said they wouldn't get off me until I took back what I said in fourth grade. "What was that?" I wheezed.

"Like you don't remember," Buzz scoffed.

"All that stuff about George Armstrong Custer," growled Max. I told them they would have to tell me what it was so I could take it back.

Buzz said, "Just say 'I love Custer,' and we'll let you go."

By now their weight had about collapsed my lungs, and I barely had the breath to say a thing. "I love custard," I managed, going easy on the *d*. Max said I had to say it again, and I did, and then Cal said I had to say it again, and I did. Each time I went easy on the *d*. Finally they said that was enough times. They got off me, and I was at the entrance of a cave. It looked familiar.

"No guts, no glory," Quinn said, and he wriggled inside. I crawled in behind him and right away fell onto some rocks. Quinn had gone ahead, and I ran to keep up. "We won't go very far," he said, but he was lying. A couple of more corners and it was pitch-dark. "We don't need flashlights," he declared, and it was true. I could see, just barely. We continued into the darkness, wading through pools of black water. I had a raging thirst and cupped some water into my mouth.

Quinn scooped up some cave water with his palm and looked at it close. He said it was full of bugs, and I told him to quit joking around. I filled my own palm and took a look. Bugs, sure enough. They had antennas like saw blades and mouths like octopus beaks. "Don't get 'em in your nostrils," Quinn advised. "They'll go for your brain." With that I found myself on the shore of Pactola Lake.

Out in the middle of the lake, a motorboat was slowly going back and forth, back and forth. It looked familiar. I squinted and recognized the *Corpse Hunter*. I didn't see any fishing poles. A guy showed up at my elbow—it was Curly, the worm grunter. I asked if he knew what was going on. Curly said they were dragging for a corpse, somebody named Fred.

Suddenly I was back on the lake bottom again, searching for my backpack. This time I definitely had it spotted and swam for it fast as I could. The prize was nearly in my grasp when a giant hook came out of nowhere and dragged it away.

Maybe it was the image of the coroner's drag hook that did it. Suddenly I was back in my worst nightmare, the one I'd been having for years. Everybody thought I was dead, only I wasn't. I was in the morgue and on my back, on the marble slab. The lights were blinding. I couldn't cry out, couldn't move a muscle. The Carvers' father, dressed in green hospital scrubs, was leaning over me, peering at me through those strange glasses of his, extra thick with lenses that magnified his eyeballs. He was staring at me like a piece of meat. Over his shoulder, all sorts of gruesome instruments hung on the wall.

My nightmare was going where it always went. The coroner leaned closer, scalpel in one hand, huge clamps in the other. The stench of his tobacco breath washed over me. With all my might, I tried to move a muscle, if only to twitch, to blink, to do something—anything.

I couldn't, and down came the scalpel to open up my chest.

That's when, like so many times before, I frightened myself awake. It was a little after 3:00 by the red numbers on my desk clock. Across the room, Quinn was snoring softly.

I lay there in a cold sweat, my body so filled with electricity, it felt like I was a short-circuiting toaster. Me being me, I was trying to keep it to myself and not cry out. Suddenly I froze up, like I'd gotten unplugged. I couldn't feel a thing. I tried to sit up, but it was three degrees beyond impossible. I couldn't twitch a finger. Couldn't even blink. I was scared out of my mind but I kept telling myself not to go crazy. Just hang on, it'll pass, it'll pass. If I hadn't been able to see, hadn't heard Quinn's breathing and the wind in the pines outside, my mind would have come unhinged.

When I was finally able to move again, the clock said 3:45. For thirty-some minutes, I'd been completely paralyzed. I sat up, put my feet on the floor, tried standing up. Everything seemed to work.

I got back in bed, curled up on my side, and fell sound asleep. When I woke, I felt like I'd been mauled by a bear. I couldn't remember a worse night in my entire life. The nightmare about being mistaken for dead, I could live with that. I'd been living with it for years. The part about being paralyzed—had that really happened, or had I dreamed that part, too?

Quinn was already awake. He was sitting on the edge of his bed and pulling on his jeans. "I didn't know you were such a thrasher," he said. "You kept mumbling something about Custer. What was that all about?"

"Custard," I said.

"That's kind of unusual."

Suddenly I could see the way to get past the tension of the night before and get us back on track. "Hey, Quinn," I said. "Are you still up for exploring the Halls of the Dead?"

"Are you?"

"What's the use of discovering a cave if you aren't going to explore it?"

"You aren't spooked by it anymore?"

"I dreamed about it last night. We could even see in the dark—that must mean something."

"Maybe *you'll* be able to. I think I'll bring along some serious illumination."

Attila, Go Home

WE WOLFED DOWN SOME breakfast and were out the door in half an hour. This time we jumped on our mountain bikes instead of our road bikes. We'd need them for where we were going.

Half a mile down the Mickelson Trail, we passed the foot of the Carvers' driveway. Attila was there again, on the lookout, almost like he was waiting for us.

Just like before, the war dog fell in alongside me. "Go home!" I yelled. "Attila, go home!"

Nothing doing.

"He'll peel off," Quinn said. "Don't pay any attention to him."

Attila didn't peel off. He followed us all the way into Custer and whined when we went into the Wal-Mart to buy the "serious illumination" Quinn was after. We bought headlamps to rig on our bike helmets and lantern flashlights to hold in our hands.

By now I'd run out of allowance money, but Quinn was still flush from busing dishes. I told him I'd pay him back. His reply: "Fuhgeddaboudit."

From the checkout, we could see Attila waiting outside the sliding doors. Craftily, we exited the back of the building. From there we sneaked around the side and practically tiptoed to the bike racks. Wouldn't you know, the war dog was keeping an eye on our bikes from the front entrance. He bounded over to us and planted himself at my feet with a "What's next?" expression on his face. I asked Quinn if he thought we should call the Carvers.

"There goes our day if you do. This dog's way smart. He knows how to get home. I still think he'll peel off, but if he doesn't, what does it really matter?"

We made another stop at a convenience store, for bottled water, Gatorade, and snacks. Just west of Custer, with Attila still sticking like glue, we left the pavement and charged up a dirt Forest Service road.

Logging had fallen off in the Black Hills, but the roads left behind make it easy to get just about anywhere. We'd discovered the cave the summer before while messing around at the headwaters of French Creek. As the crow flies, the entrance was only five miles from home.

The riding began to get steep, and for some reason, I started feeling the pain. Quinn was opening up a good lead on me, and not because I was letting him. In fact, I kept trying to keep up. I could feel the strength draining from my legs like water out of a leaky bucket. My windpipe was burning. My lungs couldn't get enough air. I was glad I had my inhaler in my pocket. I might have had to use it.

Quinn looked back from time to time, but never slowed up. Maybe he thought I was faking it. Finally I couldn't see him anymore. I kept riding as best I could, the war dog close by my side and running as tirelessly as ever. It almost seemed like he was wondering why I was having trouble.

The punishment continued until I finally caught up with Quinn. He was waiting in the shade of a big ponderosa. He had found the spot where we had to start walking.

I pulled in, gulping air, dismounted, and went to ground. Quinn's smile was full of doubts. "What's up with you?"

"You blistered me, that's what. You were merciless."

"C'mon, you were doggin' it. Quit pretending, Brady, you coulda blown by me anytime."

"I'm tellin' you, I was out of gas. Maybe I'm losing it. Fine by me if I am."

"I thought you said the buzzing didn't really hurt. So what's the problem?"

"Problem? Quinn, I've been infected by germs from outer space."

"*Infected! Germs!* What are you talking about?

Germs are *bad* bacteria. What you've got is more like the kind the professor told us about, the ones that help you digest food. Your bacteria are a gift no one else has. They make it possible for you to be incredible. You aren't talking about going to see the doctor, are you?"

"Are you kidding? They'd put me in quarantine for weeks, months, maybe even years, until they developed an antibiotic that could kill off space germs."

"There you go again."

"Okay, space bacteria. I wouldn't be playing any basketball, that's for sure."

"Quarantine . . . you're onto something there. The government would keep you in some high-tech containment bubble, and we'd never even know where. Probably at some secret base in Nevada. You're right, we shouldn't tell anybody about your microbes, not even the professor."

"I wasn't thinking I would."

"Meanwhile, if nature has dealt you a winning hand, you might as well play it. Instead of hoping it's gone away, you should be hoping it's only recharging its batteries."

Right then I thought about telling Quinn about my freeze-up episode during the night, but I wasn't sure I hadn't dreamed it, and he didn't want to hear about it anyway. I got some Gatorade out of my pack, sat in the shade for a few minutes, and drank it down. "I've got my wind back," I announced. "Onward!"

As we were stashing the bikes in the trees, I tried

telling Attila to wait behind with them, but of course he wouldn't. We hiked across a mountainside that had burned back in the summer of 2000. The forest fire started near Jewel Cave and torched about 85,000 acres. It skipped over the draw where we'd found the Halls of the Dead.

We had a landmark in mind, a giant ponderosa shaped like a slingshot that would help us find the entrance to our cave. If the distant face of Crazy Horse lined up perfectly in the fork of the pine, you were almost there.

It was rough picking our way across the burn, through all the timber the wind had brought down. I thought it would be even rougher for Attila, but he turned out to be nimble as a cat.

We took a rest with a panoramic view—Crazy Horse to the northeast, the town of Custer below us to the east, and beyond the town, French Creek winding across Custer State Park and into the rolling prairies. Attila stayed at my side. I stroked the crown of his head; he licked my face. "That's a Carver you're petting," Quinn pointed out.

"I know. I can't believe it." I poured some water out of one of my bottles, and Attila lapped it up in midair.

Blink, and from this spot, you could see Custer's column advancing up French Creek in July of 1874, two summers before the Battle of the Little Bighorn. He brought a thousand men along on his camping trip into the Hills, ten companies of horse soldiers and two of infantry. They had a hundred and fifty wagons loaded with supplies and five hundred beef cattle for fresh meat.

The expedition included two miners and a geologist. Custer brought them along in case of any discoveries of gold they weren't supposed to be looking for—wink, wink. Find gold they did, and Custer sent a man on horseback to speed the news to the nearest telegraph station. Hordes of gold seekers poured into the Black Hills, off-limits since the treaty signed only six years earlier had promised it to the Sioux for "as long as the rivers run and grass grows, and trees bear leaves." Three years after Custer's expedition, their sacred Black Hills, and a whole lot more, were taken away from them.

"Hey, Brady, I can see the wheels turning. What's on your mind?"

"History."

"Well, let's go make some."

We were getting close to the cave. The adrenaline began to pump, and I jumped ahead of Quinn. I even found our marker tree, the big ponderosa with the view of Crazy Horse's distant face through the fork.

The entrance to our cave was just as we'd left it, a small hole in the mountainside camouflaged by a leaning tree and an overhanging rock. A strong wind was rushing out of the Halls of the Dead. My fear of the place came rushing back, too. I could feel it in the roots of my teeth.

I had to get ahold of myself. I have too much cave experience, I told myself, to be this afraid. We both did, and Quinn would be with me. We'd been in Wind Cave together, Jewel Cave, Rushmore Cave, and Sitting Bull Crystal Caverns.

As we kicked off our hiking boots and pulled on our warm clothes, we weren't saying a thing. Even Quinn seemed real nervous. All that caving you're talking about, I reminded myself, was on guided tours. This isn't going to be anything like a guided tour.

We sat down and put our boots back on, double-tying the laces. My mind was going a mile a second. The guys who discovered those famous caves, do you think they were members of some caving club? No way, they were guys like us. Go big or go home, Brady.

All the while, I was hoping Quinn was questioning our sanity. We hadn't even left a note back home about where we were going.

Stop it, I told myself. What are the chances an accident would happen to both of us?

By now we were pulling on our rain gear, tops and bottoms. The only thing we remembered for sure about our cave was that it was cold and damp. We rigged our headlamps onto our bike helmets, pulled on our gloves, and threw on our backpacks. After losing mine at the lake, I'd brought along my old one, ratty but serviceable. "What about Attila?" I asked.

"He's not crazy enough to follow us inside."

"I'm not so sure."

"What does it matter? You ready?" Quinn's jaw was clenched, but he sounded a little shaky.

"Ready as I'll ever be." We flicked on our lights, and Quinn slithered inside, supple as a snake. I wriggled in after him.

Behind us, Attila had only his head inside the entrance and was whining something awful. "Stay," I ordered. "You got the right idea. Stay, Attila!"

The war dog wasn't about to be left behind. In he came.

The Halls of the Dead

ATTILA AT MY SIDE, I waited inside the mouth of the cave as Quinn scrambled down the slope, all strewn with loose rock, into the Halls of the Dead. From the murky landing below, Quinn motioned for me to follow. I remembered how much I hadn't enjoyed being here, in the cold and the dark and the confinement, nobody knowing where we were.

Attila's ears were on alert, and the hair along his spine was standing up. He was looking at me like, Are you sure about this?

I started down. Attila whined, and then he followed.

"So far, so good," Quinn said. "This is as far as we could get the first time. Then we came back the next day with those junky flashlights and got a little farther."

I pointed my big lantern flashlight down the cramped

tunnel leading out of the landing. Water was dripping from the ceiling to a muddy floor. "I remember," I said. "The second time we got to a small room where we could stand up."

Quinn led the way into the low passage. Our bike helmets crunched and scraped whenever they struck the ceiling. "How you doing?" Quinn called over his shoulder. From behind me Attila whined as if in answer.

"I wish our headlamps gave more light, so we could put these flashlights away in our packs. It'd be better to have both hands free."

"The headlamps are more for playing cards in a tent, I guess."

No whining, I thought as Quinn got going again. Leave that to Attila. You got yourself into this, so suck it up.

At last we made it to the room we remembered. It was no bigger than my parents' walk-in closet. "From here on," Quinn declared, "it's all uncharted territory." Quinn pointed his beam into the passage leading deeper into the cave. The tunnel was narrower than the one we'd come through. "How does it look to you?"

Like the entrance to a tomb, I thought. "Like the gut of a snake," I replied.

Quinn stooped low and led onward. We followed the passage as it wound back and forth like a sidewinder, up and down like a roller coaster. With all the duck walking, my backbone felt like it was breaking. Quinn stopped for a rest, finally, at a dry rock as flat as a park bench. My Achilles tendons were tight as bowstrings.

Attila wasn't so anxious anymore. He lay down beside me and rested his head on his paws. "Don't you wish you had his coat?" I asked Quinn. "All these layers I'm wearing, and the cold's pouring right through."

Quinn tugged at his chin strap and pointed his light down the tunnel. "We're cold because we stopped. The answer is to keep moving."

As we started out again, the passage began to widen. Before long we had standing room, a huge relief. I stopped to rest, but Quinn sped ahead like he was on an Easter egg hunt. His lights turned a corner and disappeared. If he hit a dead end, it would've been fine by me. I was still feeling weak. We could call it good and head for home.

Was Quinn waiting or was he on the move? I stopped and listened. Attila held his breath, too. We heard faint footfalls. I got going and hustled to catch up. When Attila and I finally did, Quinn was standing still like he'd been turned to stone.

He didn't say a thing, just let me come up beside him and shine my light around. "Stay back, Attila," I warned. We were standing above a room three or four times bigger than my house. "How's this for a discovery!" Quinn cried, and slapped me on the back.

"Major discovery," I agreed. The cavern below, damp and dripping, was exquisite and fantastic beyond belief. It had hundreds upon hundreds of stalagmites, stalactites, and much more: columns, formations that hung like draperies, freestanding sculptures of smooth white stone. I was glad, after all, that I'd talked myself into this craziness.

"It needs a name, Brady."

"Palace of the Dead King."

"Perfect."

"You hungry, Quinn?"

"Let's dine in the palace."

We found a way down through enormous blocks of limestone fallen from the ceiling. The blocks weren't covered with calcite like the rest of the cavern, maybe because they'd fallen recently. I pointed my beam at the ceiling and saw fractures among blocks that hadn't come down yet. If one of those things broke loose, it could crush a T-rex.

Out in the middle of the palace floor, we sat on a marble slab of white flowstone with a high back to it that looked uncannily like a throne for our dead king. He must have been something of a giant. We pulled out our lunch. It didn't take long to devour the pb&js we'd slapped together at home, two apiece. Quinn was amused when I gave one of mine to Attila. "What is it with you two? It's like a boy and his dog, only he's not yours."

"Beats me what's gotten into him. Let's explore the palace."

We discovered four passages leading out. We knew they went places because every one had a strong airflow. It was mind-boggling to try to imagine the complexity of passages in this one layer of limestone, like cracks running every which way through a shattered windshield.

One of the passages had standing room. Five minutes down it, we made out the eerie, faraway sound of running water.

Twenty yards farther on, we started down an incline. The sound of the ever-louder water led us on. The pitch got steeper. "Don't slip," Quinn said. As the rush of water became a roar, Quinn froze in his tracks at a threshold of pure blackness. "Careful," he said. "There's room for you to stand right beside me, but nowhere else." I inched my way toward him, Attila close on my heels.

I told Attila to keep back and he did. As I joined Quinn, I found myself above a gaping pit. It had to be eighty feet across. Halfway around to the left, the waterfall we'd been hearing shot out of a hole in the wall and dropped a hundred feet or more into the pit's inky waters. "Another huge discovery," Quinn said. "Let's call it the Abyss of Hades."

"You nailed it."

We were standing on a ledge that made almost a complete circle around the top of the pit. Quinn ran his beam around the right side of the ledge, and I added mine. Halfway around the circle was the mouth of a tunnel. "We can explore that if we can reach it," Quinn said.

The ledge between us and the tunnel was littered with broken rock. It was also slick with dripping water. At its narrowest, the ledge was about two feet wide.

"That's doable," Quinn said.

Why push it? I thought, but what I said was "I guess so, as long as we don't slip. The ledge kind of tilts down."

"No way we're gonna slip. You could do it in your sleep."

I pointed my beam into the pit. The utter blackness all but swallowed the light. If we fell in, there'd be no climbing out. We would tread water until the cold killed us, which wouldn't take long. "Must be a sinkhole," I said. "Like that one all those Ice Age mammoths down at Hot Springs fell into and couldn't get out of. If we fall in, it's going to be a mammoth mistake."

"Good one, Brady, but think how many mammoths went to the edge and *didn't* fall in. Remember, our dads explored abandoned gold mines around Lead when they were teenagers, which is way more extreme than this. Those old mines can cave in at any second. Stay where you are. I'll go first."

I pointed my lantern beam at Quinn's footing as he started along the ledge around the right side of the pit. Step by careful step, he made it all the way. "No problem!" he called over the roar of the waterfall.

"My turn," I said without a whole lot of confidence. I turned around and looked at the dog. "Attila, am I actually going to do this?"

Attila barked. Whether that was intended as warning or encouragement, I couldn't tell.

Quinn kept his beam trained on the ledge in front of

me. I visualized every step I would have to make. "Here goes nothing," I said, and started across. I had to make myself keep breathing. I'd never concentrated so hard in all my life.

I was halfway across when it happened. I slipped. Just slipped, and my flashlight went flying. With a yell, I went over the edge, or half of me did. I was on my stomach and sliding down, losing inches every second. Pretty quick, all I had left on the ledge was my elbows, forearms, and fingers. I probed with my feet for something to step on, but there was nothing underneath me but air.

My body weight was pulling me down, and I lacked the strength to pull myself up. Quinn was working his way back to me, but he wasn't going to make it in time. "I'm coming!" Quinn yelled. "Just hang on!"

Can't last that long, I thought. "Attila!" I cried. "C'mon, boy, come here, Attila."

Attila whined, then crept closer. Quinn could see what I already knew—the dog was my only chance. Quinn kept his light trained on us. It was getting impossible to hang on any longer.

My eyes met Attila's. He knew what I wanted, but he was afraid, and retreated a little. I was sure I was done, but then he moved closer yet and leaned down to me. I grabbed that big spiked collar of his, grabbed and hung on with one hand and then both.

Which left us both stuck in limbo. I was dangling above that bottomless pit, and it was all Attila could do to hold his ground.

The pull of the void became stronger and stronger, irresistible as a black hole in deep space. I heard claws scraping on wet stone. Attila was slipping. I took a sudden drop, and he almost came over the edge. I was dragging him down with me.

With a fierce glint in his eye, the war dog began to pull with a power that defied understanding. He put it into reverse and dragged me up and over and onto the safety of the ledge.

On my hands and knees, Quinn's light on us all the while, I followed Attila back to safety. I lay there trembling and gasping, completely spent, as Quinn traversed the slippery rim of the sinkhole and finally joined us. "That was insane, Brady!"

"My inhaler," I wheezed. "It's in my backpack—outside pocket. I feel a bad one coming on."

"All that strength you got from Fred, it really *is* gone." Quinn found my inhaler for me and I brought it to my mouth. Three or four puffs, and my airway began to open up.

Either the medicine held off the attack, or this wasn't asthma. Terror could have accounted for it. "Man I'm cold," I said, and struggled trembling to my feet. "Let's get out of here, Quinn."

A thunderstorm greeted us as we emerged from the Halls of the Dead. Rain never felt so good. We were back in the world, back among the living.

We hustled across the mountainside and through the down timber in the rain. Unfortunately, my encounter

with Fred's microbes didn't seem to be over. My fingertips and my toes and the tips of my ears and my nose
were buzzing again, painfully this time. Even worse,
they were going numb, which was new. I slipped and
fell. As I got to my feet, Attila sniffed my hands, whatever that was about.

The rain quit just as we got to our bikes. We stripped
off our muddy rain gear and put it away. It was early
evening. Mount Harney and the Needles were under the
span of a huge rainbow. "Sorry about what happened
back there," Quinn said. "I didn't know when to quit.
We came this close to losing you."

"That'll be our secret," I said. "Forget it."

"I don't think I ever will."

"Well, we lived through it. 'All's well that ends well,'
right?"

We jumped on the bikes and put the hammer down.
In Custer, we ate burgers at the Purple Pie Palace. Attila
waited outside where he could keep an eye on me
through the screen door.

It was getting dark, almost 9:00, as we neared home.
Attila peeled off at the Carvers' driveway. "Thanks for
saving my life," I told him. "You're stronger than I ever
would have guessed." My new friend cocked his head
and looked at me quizzically, then bounded for home.

20

Promise Me One Thing

THE SILENCE AS WE opened the door to my house felt
spooky, at least to me. My dad would be gone for a
couple more days with Uncle Jake. I found myself missing the rest of the family way over in Iowa.

I took a casserole from the freezer and we heated it
up. After we ate, Quinn wanted to shoot some hoops by
the yard light. I think he wanted to see if I could still
dunk. I was pretty sure I couldn't. "How are you feeling?" he asked.

"Weird."

"What do you mean, 'weird'?"

"Just, weird." I didn't want to tell him about the
numbness, which was getting worse. It was traveling up
my arms and legs.

"Like, sick?"

"Not really."

"Good."

Even my scalp was starting to feel numb. Fred's microbes were definitely doing something new. Not knowing what was going to happen next was getting scary. I let my mind run, and it landed in a horrifying place.

I remembered that we had some antibiotic pills upstairs, from when I'd gotten strep back in January. Chances might be slim to none that they would work against germs from Mars, but I might as well give them a try. I went upstairs and took two. I came downstairs looking pretty worried, not even trying to hide it. I guess I was ready to talk. "What's the matter?" Quinn asked.

I shrugged and said, "I've just come up with a wild paranoid theory about what's going on."

"Well, what is it?"

"Okay, it goes like this. Maybe I was right—whatever I got from Fred really *is* an infection."

"Go on."

"Let's say it's a disease, and it goes through different stages. In the early stages, the extremophile bacteria go wild and infect every cell in your body, and that gives you—how would I describe it—*supercapability*."

"Good word . . . Carry on."

"Your immune system reacts by mounting a counterattack."

"Sounds likely. Then what?"

"The alien extremophiles protect themselves by going dormant."

"Like they were dormant for millions of years while Fred was flying around in space?"

"Yeah, like that. Here's the worst part of my theory. The last couple days, the alien microbes have been exchanging genetic information with every cell in my body. So, in the stage that's coming, it's not only Fred's microbes that are going to go dormant. They're going to take me with them."

"Let me get this straight. You're afraid you're going to go dormant for millions of years?"

"I'm just trying to visualize the stages. Tell me what's wrong with my theory."

"It might be a little far-fetched. I mean, what are the odds you're going to go dormant?"

"Or dead . . ."

Quinn yawned a huge yawn. "Somehow I doubt you're going to wake up dead tomorrow, Brady. You always did have an overactive imagination. Seems more likely Fred's 'crobes are just feeling wimpy, kind of sitting out a quarter on the bench. Tomorrow morning they'll be back in the game, and you'll be slammin' and jammin'. Girls will be tearing the shirt off your back."

"Just promise me one thing, Quinn."

"You look all serious all of a sudden."

"I *am* serious. Let's say the Martian bacteria win out, and I go totally dormant."

"'Totally dormant'—what would that look like?"

"Maybe it would look like death. That's what I'm afraid of."

"That would be insane. You mean, everybody would think you were dead, only you really wouldn't be, you'd only be dormant."

"Hello, that's what I've been saying. I wouldn't be totally dead."

"If I was in your shoes, I sure wouldn't want to get cremated."

"Or get an autopsy."

"An autopsy on a live guy. That's just grotesque, Brady."

"Maybe so, but stick with this a minute. Let's say I die in my sleep."

"Quit talking like that, dude!"

"Let me finish. You know they'd do an autopsy to find out the cause."

"They'd probably figure it was your asthma."

"They'd cut me open to make sure. While I was still alive."

"You're creeping me out."

"Take a wild guess who would be dissecting me."

"Old man Carver! What a nightmare, Brady!"

"I know. Actually, I've been having that nightmare for years."

"Holding out on me, eh? Tell me about it."

I knew I was ready to spill this awful stuff, and I launched into the scary details. I had his attention. My cousin was enjoying this like you would a good horror show, and he never interrupted.

"Awesome," he said when I was done. "That was

strangely weird, terribly twisted, and horrifically bizarre. You know what, I always thought you had it made down here in Hill City. Your thing with the Carvers is deeper than I ever guessed."

"So I want you to promise me one thing, Quinn."

"Okay, I promise. Now tell me what it is."

"If this suddenly gets me, and I go down, and everybody agrees I'm stone-cold dead, you won't let old man Carver do an autopsy."

"Not *let* him? He's the coroner."

"You'll find a way, no matter what. Promise?"

"I already did."

"Promise again."

"You got it," Quinn said. "No matter what it takes, I will not under any circumstances let Daddy Carver—or anyone else for that matter—cut you open, on account of how you might only be dormant. Is that good enough?"

"Thanks. Now I can rest easy."

"But not in peace, you doofus."

"I think I'll crash. I'm wasted beyond words."

"I'm glad you've finally run out of them. Before you go to sleep, I suggest you turn off your mind."

"I'll try," I assured him. With that, I dragged myself upstairs, literally. My legs were pretty much numb. I looked over my shoulder. Quinn hadn't been watching me go, or he would've asked why I was lurching like Frankenstein. He had the TV on.

Soon as I lay down, it was like I'd grabbed hold of a high-voltage electrical wire. It flipped me from my side onto my back. For good measure, here came a bolt like lightning that seared me through and through. Then it shut off. I lay there stiff as a beetle in a bug collection. Here it comes, I thought. The dormancy.

The sensation that came next is almost impossible to explain. It felt like every cell, every atom in my body was being rearranged, melted down and rearranged. Maybe it was something like when a caterpillar spins a cocoon and then breaks itself down into goo, before its metamorphosis. The only question was, What was next?

Introducing Destructo

WHAT CAME NEXT WAS the morning, waking up like normal and finding myself among the living. "You survived the night," Quinn observed with a grin. He was taking waffles out of the toaster oven.

I thought about filling him in on the new and horrible things that had happened, but I was all confused. Maybe it was over. "Give me five, I'm still alive," I joked instead.

When it came to my health, I'd always been secretive as a ferret. It about killed me once to ask a pharmacist what to do about athlete's foot. I wouldn't have, except it was driving me so crazy I was considering amputation.

Quinn grabbed the syrup and went to chowing down on his waffles. I detected a smirk. He thought I was an amusing case, all right.

The phone rang and I jumped for it. I hoped it was Wyoming or Iowa calling. Turned out it was next door, the Carvers. It was Buzz. "Hey, Brady, guess what?"

"What, Buzz?"

"We found your backpack yesterday afternoon, on the bottom of Pactola. Snagged it with my dad's drag hook."

"I kind of thought you might give that a try," I said cautiously.

"No wonder your backpack went down so fast, eh, Brady?"

I didn't say a thing, just waited.

"We've been to the museum. We even talked to the meteorite expert, Dr. Rip. He said you didn't even tell him you'd lost it."

"I couldn't stand to."

"It's valuable, right?"

"I guess so."

"You guess so? He said it's from Mars! First you were holding out on us about it being a meteorite, and now we find out it's from Mars and worth a boatload of money!"

I hesitated, wondering where to go from here. I was glad it wasn't Mean Max I was talking to. With Buzz there was always a chance he'd cut me some slack. "Thanks a lot," I said. "I really appreciate you guys finding it for me."

"Hey, not so fast, Brady. We've got just as solid a claim as you do. Haven't you heard about rights of salvage? Not only that, we got possession, and possession is nine tenths of the law!"

"So . . . where *do* we go from here, Buzz?"

"Bet you expect we have to settle this in court, right?"

"I wasn't thinking that far ahead."

"That would be really lame, don't you think?"

"Totally."

"We got a much quicker way, and it'll be fair."

"How would it work?"

"Come on over and find out, you and Quinn both."

"Like, when?"

"Like how about now?"

Half an hour later we were pedaling up the Carvers' driveway. What did we have to lose? we figured. Still, I couldn't help remembering that every other time we'd gone over, for paintball or whatever, we'd come home with the short end of the stick.

Attila came charging down the driveway, as large and ferocious as a dire wolf from the Pleistocene. He was barking at first, but then he had me spotted. He ran up close and sniffed my hand. Quinn and I got off our bikes and walked them the rest of the way. I was patting Attila's head and he was wagging his tail as the twins showed up at the corner of the house. They looked pretty baffled about me and their war dog. I was remembering how they'd sat on me in my crazy dream a couple of nights before. These were really big guys.

"Come and check out our catapult," Buzz said. Max wasn't saying anything.

What about Fred? I wondered as we followed them around the side of the house. Quinn, I could see, was wondering the same thing. Hadn't they called us to come over and settle about the meteorite?

Soon as we got out back, their catapult loomed larger than life, no less than twenty feet high, at the near end of the meadow. Quinn was seeing it for the first time and was having trouble believing his eyes. In another strange twist, Cal was sitting on a commode at the foot of the medieval war machine, with his fist to his chin like the famous statue I couldn't remember the name of.

Silent Cal got up and wandered off to the side. He hadn't been doing any business, just sitting on the lid. Five or six other toilets were scattered around, along with a lot of other junk.

Buzz was busting his buttons. "Introducing Destructo!" he boomed with a sweeping gesture. Max's pride was more fierce, like he was going to put the hurt on us if we didn't react properly.

Quinn gave it up for Destructo. "That's just insane!" he cried.

Max nodded with satisfaction. Buzz beamed.

"Colossal!" I added, but they didn't make like they'd heard. What else was new? Quinn's reaction was all that counted. Quinn had always gotten a pass, maybe just for being from Lead. Their teams had a raft of state titles. I was always going to be chopped liver on account of my Custer report back in fourth grade.

We walked closer yet to their wicked-looking new

toy. The monstrosity was constructed mostly out of black steel. It was mounted on wheels, like a Trojan horse. It crossed my mind to wonder if my house was out of range. Buzz asked if I remembered the scale model they'd built for school.

I laughed. "Are you kidding? You guys nailed the principal with that golf ball."

"We forgot to yell 'Fore!' Fortunately he was cool about it."

"Does it work?"

"We'll find out in a few minutes. You guys are pretty special. You get a sneak preview this morning, and we aren't even going to charge you admission."

The twins marched us over to the catapult and invited us to take a seat. We did, on the two closest toilets, and Max sat down on a third. Buzz told us they'd found them at the dump. "We found a lot of throw-ables there, these bowling balls, that cash register, those kitchen sinks, those computers, that old outboard motor . . ."

Quinn pointed off to the left. "What's up with the pile of stones?" More than a few, I noticed, were the same kind of river cobbles missing from my mother's flower beds.

"We're going to hurl thirty or forty at a time. Better hope they don't shred your house, Brady!"

Off to the side, Silent Cal was chewing on a piece of grass. He took off his cowboy hat and swiped a grasshopper from his pant leg. We said hi. Cal flicked his eyes at us in vague recognition.

Max stood up tall and cleared his throat, like he was about to give a speech. At the same time, Buzz sat down. Even Attila wondered what was going on. Max wasn't known as an orator.

"Here goes," Max began with his trademark growl. "Picture you're back in the 1300s, safe, sound, and filthy rich in your castle. An army of fifty thousand marches up and camps outside your walls. They want to get inside. You know why? They want to tear you limb from limb along with all your relatives and servants. You wonder why they're chopping down a bunch of your trees. Day by day you watch helplessly as they build a siege catapult like this one, only theirs is made out of wood. How would you feel?"

"Terrified?" I suggested.

"You got it, Steele. The attackers start off by hurling rocks and boulders, but that gets old. The longer the siege, the more interesting it gets. They capture your cattle and horses, and hurl big hunks of them over the walls at you. Your wife gets killed by incoming fire—a flying sheep. Watch out, here come some blazing hot irons and casks of flaming pitch. They grab the messenger you sent for help and hurl his head back in at you. How'd you like to get hit by a human head, somebody you know?"

Quinn applauded. "Max, you ought to write this stuff down. Don't let it get away from you."

"Thanks, Quinn, I did put some work into it. Now,

for the construction details, I'll turn it over to Buzz."

The twins switched places. "What you guys are looking at," Buzz began, "is basically two steel A-frames braced to support a lever on a fulcrum. The hurling arm is the lever. Notice that it has a counterweight—that's a ton of pig iron, by the way—suspended from one end. Don't ask me where we got the pig iron, okay?"

We nodded obediently. Attila came over and lay down beside me. Max looked hostile about that, but he didn't say anything. "Cal was our welder," Buzz went on. "He learned welding in a program the Sheriff's Department put him into while he was on probation. If he hadn't gotten into trouble, you wouldn't be looking at Destructo today. Cal's thinking of paying them back by sacking the Sheriff's Department. Just kidding. We'll probably sack Hill City instead. Any questions so far?"

I pointed to a huge hole off to our left, with fresh dirt piled all around. It was so big and so deep they could've buried a pickup in it. "What's the excavation about?"

"It's got nothing to do with the catapult," Max snapped. "Attila's been digging it. We don't know what's got into him—he's been acting weird, even running off, which he never does."

Wait a second, I thought, and then I knew. I knew exactly what had gotten into Attila. That first morning, he'd had Fred in his mouth a good long while. *He'd gotten infected.* As for him sniffing my hand and so on, somehow he knew I had the same thing he did. Now I understood how he was able to pull me up and out of the Abyss.

Buzz cleared his throat. "Let's get back to the construction. Direct your attention to the end of the hurling arm opposite the one with the counterweight. See the sling hanging from it? You attach your payload to the sling. Your payload weighs hardly anything compared to your counterweight. What you've got now is a seesaw with a rabbit sitting on one end and an elephant on the other. Pull the trigger, and your rabbit's gonna fly. Any further questions?"

We shook our heads. Still no mention of Fred.

"Okay, then. Party on like the Dark Ages!"

A Simple Contest

THE CARVER BOYS SWUNG into action. They attached
a cable to the unweighted end of Destructo's hurling arm and began to crank on a winch. Bit by bit,
as they spelled each other, the one-ton counterweight on
the other end of the siege catapult was lifted high into
the air.

The sling attached to the lighter end was now low
enough to reach. Cal selected a bowling ball and placed
it inside. "Locked and loaded," he reported.

Suddenly, the tension was thick. The Carvers are a
prideful bunch, and this was going to be an embarrass-
ment if their demo fizzled. Max directed our attention
down the meadow, where they'd painted a big bull's-eye
on a propped-up sheet of plywood. Buzz informed us that
the target was a hundred yards away. It was just to give

them something to shoot at for the time being. Pretty soon they were going to replace it with goalposts.

Buzz had us step close for an inspection of the triggering device. He talked us through the cleverly intricate firing sequence. A crossbow was going to shoot a short length of pipe at the propped-up lid of a garbage can. When struck, the lid would pull a trip wire attached to Micro Havoc, a whole other catapult they'd built, this one only knee-high. Micro Havoc was going to hurl a baseball at a pie plate wired to a miniature guillotine. When the baseball hit the pie plate, the blade of the guillotine was supposed to drop, slicing a rope that was attached to the monster catapult's trigger mechanism.

We gave them their proper respect. You had to hand it to these guys. They didn't lack for imagination.

"Stand back!" Max thundered, and we did, way back, everybody but Cal. Just then I felt the numbness starting up in my fingertips and toes again. I went light-headed with frustration and disappointment. I'd thought my infection was gone. Here it was again, coming back strong.

Silent Cal approached the crossbow on cat's feet, as if a heavy footfall might wreak destruction on all of us. He leaned down, pulled the trigger on the crossbow, and things started happening.

The crossbow shot the piece of pipe, which hit the garbage lid dead center with a loud clang. Unhinged by the movement of the garbage lid, Micro Havoc hurled the baseball at the pie plate. Down came the guillotine as Cal sprinted to get clear.

For a second, Destructo's mighty hurling arm merely twitched. I thought we'd just witnessed a dud, but then, *WHAM!* The lengthy lever was unleashed. In a blur, the hurling arm whipsawed the air. In another blur, the bowling ball went flying down the meadow in a high, high arc, a home run ball if ever there was one. Incredibly, it way overshot the target and landed in the trees.

The Carvers celebrated with barbaric cheers, and we joined in. That would be all for today, they told us. We could come back for the public demo, soon to be announced. All the kids from the middle school and high school would be invited, and kids from Custer would be coming, too. Admission was going to be only five bucks.

We'll be back, we promised, and then we begged them to at least hurl one of the toilets for us. They gave in, loaded one up, and let it fly. A toilet sailing high above a mountain meadow is not something you see every day. It had to be one of the most beautiful things I'd seen in my life. The flying commode landed about ten yards short of the target, but that was hardly a disappointment. The impact was classic. It shattered into a hundred pieces.

We had actually started for our bikes when Buzz asked if we weren't forgetting something.

"Like what?" I asked. The numbness was moving up my arms and legs, and I was on fire to get home. This time I was going to call the doctor.

"Like, this meteorite."

Strange to say, but we'd gotten so distracted by their war machine, we'd forgotten why we came. There was Fred, right in the palm of Buzz's hand. Attila rose off his haunches and went to it like it was raw meat.

"Leave it!" Max growled. Reluctantly, Attila obeyed, eyes lasered on Fred all the while.

"Like I told you on the phone," Buzz said, "we've got a fair way to settle who owns it."

"What do you have in mind?" I asked.

"A simple contest," Buzz replied with a grin at his brothers. "We crank up Destructo and hurl the meteorite. Two from each side will go after it. The first to bring it back and set it on this toilet, right here, wins for his side."

"Sounds fair," I agreed, "as long as there's no tackling or take-away or stuff like that."

"Good point," Quinn put in. "The first one to grab the meteorite gets a free pass to the toilet."

"No problem," they agreed. "So let's do it now."

Wouldn't you know, the Carver boys made the contest even more interesting by wheeling Destructo around ninety degrees. They were going to hurl Fred into the dense stand of pines on the hillside.

The Carvers winched down Destructo's mighty hurling arm, and Cal placed Fred in the sling. Max and Buzz got their firing sequence all hair-triggered, and then Cal drew a starting line in the dirt with a sword he seemed to produce from nowhere.

We lined up, Buzz and Max together, me and Quinn together. "I'm depending on you," I whispered to Quinn. "Something's going wrong with my arms and legs. I'm buzzing and numb all over."

"It's back?"

"With a vengeance. Just remember what we talked about last night, the promise you made, okay?"

"I'm cool it with that, Brady, but you're just freaking yourself out again. It's all in your mind."

"I'll say 'Ready, aim, fire,'" Cal announced, "but that only means I'm going to start the sequence. Nobody goes until Destructo's arm snaps loose. Agreed?"

"Agreed," the four of us echoed.

"Take a deep breath," Quinn whispered.

"Wish I could," I replied.

"Okay," Cal cried. *"Ready, aim, FIRE!"*

As we watched over our shoulders, I noticed that Attila also had his eye on the sling. The war dog was lined up next to Buzz. I heard the pipe hit the garbage can lid and saw the baseball strike the pie plate. I didn't see the guillotine fall; my eyes were glued on Destructo's arm. It sprung in a wild blur and Fred went flying.

For the time being all five of us held back, eyes glued on Fred's flight. It was going to be hard enough to find him in the forest unless we had a pretty good idea how far up on the hillside to look. Fred's arc was incredibly high and incredibly long. He was much lighter than a bowling ball or a toilet. At last he fell to Earth, vanishing into the trees way up the mountainside.

"Go, go!" Cal yelled, and we all bolted. Quinn sprinted to an early lead, with Max and Buzz right on his heels. Those guys might be big, but they could run like racehorses.

At the head of the pack, fast as an arrow, sped Attila. A few seconds later the war dog charged into the trees, and I lost sight of him.

"Go, Quinn!" I cried, hobbling behind the best I could.

By the time I reached the trees, I was pretty well finished. I staggered far enough to reach a patch of shade, found a log, and got down.

I had a swooning sensation, and I braced on the log with both hands. The numbness even had ahold of my lips and my tongue. Next came the lightning bolt like the one the night before, but even more powerful. I felt myself melting down again into the goo.

I collapsed. My lights went out.

I Know You're in There

WHEN I CAME TO, I was lying flat on my back and looking up at a white ceiling. I was stiff as a board but my back didn't hurt. Nothing hurt. I couldn't feel a thing. A spider was walking across the ceiling. The lights were extremely bright. I tried to shut my eyes, but I couldn't. I couldn't even blink.

I tried to look to the side, but I couldn't.

I tried to move my fingers, my toes, my arms, my legs. There wasn't any feeling. I couldn't move a thing.

From my right came the sound of a door opening, then closing. Then I heard the squeak of shoes. A large man in green hospital scrubs moved through the edge of my vision.

I'm in the hospital in Custer, I thought, or else the one in Rapid City.

The green scrubs reappeared, then vanished without me catching a glimpse of the man's face. I heard the door opening and closing again.

All I had over me was a sheet. Hospitals were always cold, but strangely, I didn't feel cold. What put me in here, I wondered, my asthma?

The door was opening again. I heard hushed voices, maybe familiar, but I couldn't quite place them. Heavy footfalls were approaching. Two big guys appeared and leaned over me. They looked alike except one had dark curly hair and the other had a buzz. No wonder they sounded familiar. Buzz and Max had come to visit me in the hospital, probably sneaked into my room.

Buzz's face was all distorted. He was on the verge of crying. Even Max was all choked up. It hit me that I must be really bad off. Finally I remembered about Fred's bacteria. My infection was back, and it was worse, much worse.

They must think I'm not going to make it.

All along, I realized, I'd gotten these guys wrong. They actually cared. All this time, the only thing I'd seen was that they would never cut me any slack. And what about me? Was I any different? Had I ever cut them any slack? Everybody knew it wasn't easy being a Carver.

I tried to say something, anything, but I couldn't make my mouth move. It felt like I had zero air in my lungs. Who won? I thought. Who's got Fred? And where was Quinn?

"I guess his asthma got him," Buzz said.

What do you mean, "got him"? I thought.

"Yeah, probably asthma," Max agreed. "Dad'll find out."

Dad? I thought. Dad?

Then it hit me, where I was and what they were talking about. This was no bed I was on. *It was a marble slab in the county morgue, and they thought I was dead!* Their dad was going to open me up so he could sign off on what killed me.

You idiots, I tried to scream. *You fools, I'm only dormant!*

"I hated playing him in basketball," Buzz went on. "He was fast. Deadly accurate, too, when he was on top of his game."

You should've seen me dunk!

Buzz dropped a tear on my face. I saw it fall, but I didn't feel it hit.

Even more amazingly, Mean Max was dabbing at his eyes. "Oh yeah, Brady would've made varsity his sophomore year."

Did he say 'Brady'? Max actually knows my first name?

Buzz reached down and rapped my skull a couple of times with his knuckles. "We had some fun giving him a hard time, but I have to admit, I kind of liked him."

"Yeah, me too. You have to admire him for never budging on Custer. Tell you the truth, Buzz, I don't give a hang about Custer anymore, even if there is a family connection."

"Me neither. You know what, I never could stand Custer's long hair, like in that famous photograph in our room. He's supposed to be on a military campaign, out roughing it, but here he is sitting on a big old chair in front of a big old wall tent, posing with his rifle and his Indian scouts and his hunting dogs. You get the idea he'd just been inside in front of a mirror, working on his curly locks for the camera."

"Yeah, for the newspapers back East. Remember Brady's report way back when, how Custer was a big publicity hound? That maybe he was even planning to run for president? If you think about it, all those guys he ordered into that death trap at the Little Bighorn, including our great-great-great-great-uncle or whatever he was, died because their commanding officer was a legend in his own mind. Custer sucks."

Buzz leaned down and whispered, "You hear that, Brady? Custer sucks!"

I *was* hearing it. I never thought I'd live to see the day.

Max began to pick his nose. "Weird how Brady's eyes are wide open."

"Yeah, sometimes that happens, I guess. I think Dad'll fix it before Brady's family gets here. The stare would probably spook 'em pretty bad. How many people have seen as many stiffs as we have?"

"Not many, that's for sure."

You knuckleheads! I wanted to scream, *I'm alive!*

Wait a second, I thought. Maybe I'm only having my nightmare, and it'll end like it always does.

"So, we have to make a decision, Max. Do we tell Quinn to forget it? All this crazy stuff about a disease from Mars . . . Brady's obviously dead as a doornail."

Just then I heard the door. "We told you to wait outside," Max barked.

"I had to see him!" It was Quinn's voice.

My cousin was soon at my side, leaning over me, lips trembling, scared witless. He was wearing his T-shirt that said GO BIG OR GO HOME. "My God, his eyes are open! I tell you, Brady's alive!"

Buzz shook his head. "Give it up, Quinn. They signed off on him at the hospital in Custer. He was DOA. No pulse, no brain activity, the works. What else do you need?"

"Like I told you, he's only dormant!"

Finally, I thought. Finally these guys are going to get the concept through their thick skulls.

Quinn leaned down, all wild-eyed. "I know you're in there, Brady. Hang on, just hang on. I should've paid better attention. Listen, we're gonna get you out of this place. I got ahold of Cal. He's outside waiting with his Mercury."

Max gave Quinn a poke. "Is he really, or did you just make that up to make a stiff feel better who can't hear you anyway?"

"Cal's out there, and trust me, you guys, Brady's alive! I promised him—no autopsy! I promised!"

Max ran his hand back and forth in front of my eyes, trying to get me to blink. "What did the professor say?"

"I haven't been able to reach him. I'll try again in a few minutes. It's all happened so fast, probably he hasn't even heard. No one's been able to reach Brady's father or mother either. Why can't your dad just hold off on the autopsy, at least until Brady's dad gets back from Wyoming?"

"Because he's got the green light," Buzz said, "and he doesn't like to put stuff off. I'm pretty sure he's going to do it any minute. He'll kill us if he finds you in here!"

Max checked his watch. "We're out of here, guys. Dad said he was giving us ten minutes, and that meant us, not you, Quinn. He'll be walking through that door anytime now. Let's go! Let's go!"

Quinn leaned in and took one last desperate look. I tried to squeeze out a tear. It was useless. Buzz and Max tore Quinn away, and they hurried from the room.

It was over. Quinn had tried, but what could he do?

From somewhere across the room came the sound of a slow drip. The drips came so far apart, I filled the time between them with a rising tide of panic. *Don't give up on me,* I wanted to scream. I wanted to scream it loud enough for Quinn to hear me out in the hall, outside the building, wherever he was. *Quinn, you promised!*

The door opened. Here came those squeaky shoes again, the big man in green scrubs. Old man Carver leaned over me, adjusted his glasses on his nose, peered at me through those extra-thick lenses. They magnified his eyeballs horribly. The stench of his smoker's breath washed over me. Why could I hear, see, and smell, but not feel a thing?

The coroner went away. I fought to get up. I tried to scream.

The squeak was returning. The coroner reappeared rolling a metal tray loaded with rattling instruments.

Daddy Carver leaned over, bathing me in his hideous breath. As he pulled the sheet free of my chest, I could see every blood vessel in his hideous eyes, huge like the eyes of a praying mantis. His hands, too, rubbing back and forth, were like the hands of a mantis.

The coroner pulled on latex gloves, then turned for his instruments. His praying mantis hands reappeared, scalpel in his right, clamp in his left. He leaned in, ready to make the first incision. This was the moment I had always jolted myself out of my nightmare.

Try as I might, I couldn't make it happen. There was no leaving the nightmare. This was no dream. This was really happening, and here came the scalpel . . .

"Hey, Dad!" It was Max's voice.

"What is it, son? Can't you see I'm busy?"

"We just got a line on Attila!"

The coroner turned away from my line of vision. "Oh?"

The coroner put down his instruments and went to the door. I could only hear pieces of the conversation. Max and Buzz were saying something about Attila having been seen down at Hot Springs, or Minnekahta Junction, or both.

Attila was missing, I got that much. I heard their father, all stressed, say that the autopsy could wait until tomorrow. He was going to head down to Hot Springs as fast as he could in his truck, and the boys were to head to Minnekahta Junction in Cal's Mercury. Thank goodness old man Carver was incredibly attached to that dog.

I couldn't tell what all was going on, but this much I understood: Quinn and the Carver boys had figured out how to derail the autopsy. Quinn was trying to give me a stay of execution at least until my dad got back.

A short time later—time was hard to measure— Quinn was at my side again, with Buzz and Max.

"You're out of here," Quinn whispered.

It's Not All That Great

WITH QUINN AND CAL posted as sentries, Buzz and Max loaded me onto a stretcher and whisked me out the back door of the morgue. I couldn't see a thing on account of the blanket they'd tossed over me, but I could hear what was going on. They were stuffing me into the trunk of Cal's 1970 Spoiler. As stiff as I was, they had a hard time of it.

The four of them piled into the Mercury and we headed off. Where were they going to hide me, and then what? From the trunk, everything they were saying was too garbled to make out. Had Quinn reached the professor? Had he even remembered he was going to give it another try?

I started rattling around something awful. We'd left the pavement and were onto a gravel road. When the road got even worse, all washboarded, the car started fishtailing. Cal barely slowed down.

Finally we were climbing, and Cal had to gear it down. We kept climbing. Eventually we came to a stop. Complaining about the dust, my body snatchers piled out of the car and threw open the trunk. I got the idea the stretcher poles had kept them from closing the windows.

Buzz and Max manhandled me onto the stretcher. I could see the sweet blue of the sky again. They put me down under an old ponderosa pine. I could smell the vanilla scent of the bark. High above, a squirrel leaped from branch to branch.

"So, how far's this cave?" Max growled.

"Not that far," Quinn replied.

"Better not be. You got a name for it?"

"The Halls of the Dead."

"Seriously?" asked Buzz.

"Seriously."

"Sounds like that's where Brady belongs. You ready to lift, Max?"

"Might as well start working out—football practice starts Monday. Hear that, Brady? If I get a hernia, I'm gonna kill you, ha, ha! Ready, Buzz—one, two, three, lift!"

Up I went and off through the trees, the twins huffing and grunting and complaining every step of the way. If you think this is bad, I wanted to say, wait until we get to the burned-out patch with the wind-downed timber.

Eventually we did get to the burn, and to my surprise they rose to the challenge. Getting me over every fallen tree took an incredible effort. I saw a lot of crazy angles. It was a sunny day, and the sweat was pouring off Buzz's head. "Feels like he weighs a ton!" he exclaimed.

"That's what they always say about dead guys," Max grunted.

Quinn offered to help spell the big boys with the stretcher, but they declined. At last I was no longer pitching up and down like a crab boat on the Bering Sea. "We're getting close," Quinn announced. He had the twins rest where they could sight on the face of Crazy Horse through the fork of the big ponderosa. The Carver boys talked about the time they'd been up on Crazy Horse's arm, and that blew me away. Maybe they'd secretly admired Crazy Horse all along.

They got going again, and at last they set me down in front of the Halls of the Dead. That's when I lost it. They were going to stash me inside there and walk away. They got all nervous and somber, which scared me even worse. Did any of these guys, even Quinn, actually believe I was alive?

They tried a couple of times to slide me into the cave on the stretcher. Then they grabbed hold of me, just pushed and pulled and dragged me through on my belly. They lugged me onto that first steep slope all strewn with loose rock and flipped me onto my back. The twins were panting like draft horses pulling three tons of bricks in a heat wave. "Call it good?" Buzz said.

"No way," Max grunted to my surprise. "The coyotes would smell him. We have to get Brady out of their reach."

"Good point. Coyotes are carrion eaters. That wouldn't be pretty."

Easy on the gruesome, I thought.

"I know just the place," Quinn said. Buzz and Max laid out the stretcher and rolled me onto it, facedown. At least I was on the stretcher again. They lifted me up, and down the slope we went. When we got as far as the passage with the low ceiling, the twins said they'd had enough. They set me down. I thought for sure this was the end of the line. Then they asked what the cave was like up ahead. Quinn told them we weren't very far from the Palace of the Dead King.

They really liked the name. "That's where we're taking him," Max announced. "I mean, that's perfect."

"Yeah," Buzz added, "Brady will be the dead king."

On they went through their tunnel of pain. Whenever they bumped their heads—nobody had thought to bring helmets—Max and Buzz hollered like they'd been murdered. Both were bleeding, it sounded like, but they joked about it being a tune-up for football and kept going.

"Awesome," I heard Silent Cal call from ahead. Cal and Quinn had the lights.

"What's awesome?" grunted Buzz, heaving for breath.

"Drop your load and take a look."

The twins set me down and went to see. I heard their gasps and knew they were looking into the Palace of the Dead King.

With what had to be their last reserves of brute strength, Max and Buzz stretchered me down through the giant boulders and into the Palace. Quinn directed them to the throne, the slab of limestone where we'd eaten our peanut-butter-and-jelly sandwiches. They rolled me off the stretcher onto the throne, face up, thank goodness. The twins peered down at me, getting more somber than ever.

Quinn came close and got all broken up, like this was good-bye. The tears flowed until he pulled himself away.

I wondered if Quinn was going to say a few words or something, but he never got that far. Off to the side, Silent Cal was yelling something about Attila. I tried to sort through the confusion as the other three ran in that direction, lights bouncing off the walls.

I pieced it together from the amazing things they were saying. The war dog was lying there dead in the Palace of the Dead King. Not only that, but Fred was right next to his face, like he'd dropped Fred as he collapsed. I heard all that and this also: Attila's eyes were open.

My mind raced to fill in some gaps. I hadn't known how long Attila had been missing, but now it was obvious. He'd been missing ever since Destructo hurled Fred into the woods. I'd been assuming that either the

Carvers or Quinn had found the meteorite, but neither had. With his speed and superior sense of smell, Attila had gotten there first. He must have snatched Fred and run straight to the cave. For some reason he thought that's where Fred belonged.

"How'd Attila know about your cave?" Max asked.

"Because he came in here with us," Quinn replied. "I know, we should have told you. Hey, wait a second, you guys, maybe your dog isn't dead."

"What are you talking about?" the Carver boys said at once.

"He might just be dormant, same as Brady. Let me try to explain. Remember when Attila first ran off with Fred . . ."

"Fred?"

"That's our name for the meteorite. Far Roaming Earth Diver."

"O-kay . . . ," Max said dubiously. "Go on."

"Attila had Fred in his mouth. And so did Brady, sort of, the night the meteorite crashed through his roof. He drooled all over it in his sleep. He told me so."

"O-kay . . ."

"That's how Brady got the Mars bacteria into his system. Well, Attila dropped in his tracks only a matter of hours after Brady did. The time between when the two of them dropped is probably the exact amount of time between when the two of them got infected with Fred's microbes."

"So maybe Attila's only dormant!" Buzz cried.

"That's what I'm trying to tell you, but you know what else? The professor is in danger of coming down with it, too, and real soon."

"Why him?"

"Spit! He could've got the microbes into his mouth, too. He spit on the nub off Fred's bottom!"

Cal busted out laughing. The twins joined in.

Quinn hadn't been listening to how ridiculous all of this sounded. "I'm serious, you guys! We've got to warn the professor!"

After a brief discussion as to whether or not to leave me with a flashlight—they decided against it—they took off. They left me and Attila to our terrors in the absolute darkness while they ran across the mountainside, jumped in Cal's muscle car, and sped toward Hill City to warn the professor. I could only hope that Cal wasn't going to fishtail his Mercury off the mountain and leave them all mangled five hundred feet down some boulder-strewn ravine.

There I was, flat on my back in the pitch dark for who knows how long, trying not to go stark, raving insane. At long last I detected light, then voices. The voices were those of Quinn, Cal, and the twins. But then I heard another one, and it had an English accent. They'd brought the professor.

They circled around me, lying there on the dead king's limestone slab. The professor leaned close and studied me intently. I could see his forest of ear hair and those few wisps of gray floating above his head.

Talk to me, I thought, and he did. "I don't know if you can hear me, Brady, but wouldn't it be splendid if you were merely in suspended animation?"

It's not all that great, I wanted to tell him.

"Hey, Professor," Quinn said. "What if Brady actually *is* dormant instead of dead? Could he stay dormant for millions of years, like the Martian microbes?"

"By no means, I would think. The human body is hugely complex and fragile. To begin with, it couldn't survive total dehydration."

"So, if Brady's dormant, how long does he have to live?"

"Days at most, would be my guess. Only a few days."

The professor leaned closer yet. "Brady, my lad, I've brought along a little something to squirt up your nose."

From his pocket, the professor took out a small squeeze bottle of what looked like nose spray. "It's not cold medicine," the scientist explained loudly, as if he was talking to a deaf person. "I'm only using the container."

"What is it, Dr. Rip?" inquired Buzz.

"An antidote, I hope. It killed the Martian bacteria under my microscope after a broad-spectrum antibiotic had failed. I've been experimenting around the clock, ever since I started to develop some disturbing symptoms myself, including numbness in my extremities."

"What's the antidote?" Quinn asked.

"Acetic acid—common vinegar. Here goes, Brady, a snort in each nostril. Good luck, my lad!"

With that the professor shot a mighty stream into

173

one of my nostrils and then the other. I didn't feel a thing. I waited for something to happen. The slightest result would have been nice.

Nothing happened, nothing at all.

Having almost no sense of time, I couldn't tell how long they waited for the vinegar to take effect. All too soon they were talking about leaving. On top of that, the Carvers were arguing about who Fred belonged to. "He's valuable, and he's ours," Max insisted. "We had a contest and Attila got to him first. Attila's our dog, so that settles it."

The professor heaved a sigh. "How do I make you understand? Take a look at poor Brady. I'm afraid my own infection is also rather far along—I'm getting worse as I speak. Fred's no prize. I only wish he were. Fred's a menace. I should have been much more cautious when his microbes came to life in my office. I deluded myself into thinking that the odds on them being harmful were extremely slim. It was irresponsible of me. Long odds need to be respected."

"Like getting killed by a falling tortoise," Quinn quipped. "Life is full of surprises."

"Indeed," said the professor. "I knew better."

"I don't know nothin' about no falling tortoises," said Max irritably, "and I still don't see why we should be worried. It's the spit, right, that sets it off?"

"Apparently so," Dr. Ripley agreed.

"Well then, no spit, no problem. We just want to sell the sucker."

"Oh, no!" the professor cried. "That's the last thing you should do. You have no idea what havoc might be unleashed. Listen closely to what I'm about to say. With even a slight mutation, Fred's germs might well become highly contagious. With airline travel and all, the disease that felled Brady would spread around the globe in a matter of days. Having no immunities, most if not all of humanity would perish. Billions dead, lads, including most likely yourselves."

Along about then I began to feel a tingling sensation in my fingertips, the tips of my toes, even the tips of my ears and my nose. Hope soared. Was I beginning to come out of the dormancy?

"And if I die," the professor was saying, "or go dormant, as the case may be, you must never allow Fred to leave this cave. Not for money, not for scientific study, and not for your government—they might be tempted to weaponize him for germ warfare. Not for anything or anybody."

"Just leave him in the cave?" It was Silent Cal's voice.

"Immersed in water, preferably. My experiments indicate that Fred's bacteria, for whatever reason, are neutralized by ordinary H_2O."

After a long pause, Cal called for a huddle with his younger brothers, and off they went to talk it over. I heard the professor spraying the vinegar up his own nose. "You never know," he remarked to Quinn with little hope.

When the Carver boys came back, Max stood tall and

cleared his voice. "Nobody should get Fred," he announced. "Let's flush him, like Dr. Rip said."

"I know where," Quinn volunteered.

The final resting place Quinn suggested caught their imagination. Off the five of them went to drown the space traveler in the Abyss of Hades.

By the time I saw their lights returning, I was sitting upright on the slab. I was good to go.

The sight of me stopped Quinn in his tracks. "Brady's alive!" he cried. The professor was staring at me like he couldn't believe his eyes.

They were crazy-happy to see me, not only Quinn and the professor but all three of the Carvers. All of our bad history was, well, history.

The professor marched over to Attila and squirted the remaining vinegar up his nose. We waited for the war dog to rise from his dormancy. Sure enough, he did.

How It All Came Out

As WE EMERGED FROM the cave, we realized we had a problem. What were we going to tell the outside world, including our families?

We had a lot of explaining to do.

The more we batted it around, the more obvious it became that if we told the whole story, if news of Fred and what he had done to me got out, somebody would come after us to get to the space traveler. His final resting place might not be so final after all.

"Simplicity is the key," the professor suggested. "The simpler our explanation, the better. How do we account for Brady being alive without revealing his dormancy and the microbes that made it happen?"

It was the Carver boys who came up with the solution, which turned out to be simple. They knew from their dad about true stories of people being declared dead in the hospital, only to wake up in the morgue. It had happened a bunch of times around the country and the world. Their father would buy this explanation for what had happened with me.

Max had it all figured out. "Here's our story, guys. While we were searching for Attila, Brady woke up and let himself out of the building."

"Beautiful," Buzz declared.

"I know, but I'm not done. We succeeded in finding Attila down in Minnekahta Junction. Meanwhile, Brady was walking home from the morgue. On our way back into town, we found him walking down the street in Custer. What do you think, professor?"

"Brilliant. It's a shame that a greater good has us fabricating a story, but under these extraordinary circumstances I believe it's the right thing to do. The hospital will be embarrassed to find out that Brady's asthma attack wasn't fatal, but they'll be glad they were mistaken."

There was one more thing. Fred's whereabouts needed to be accounted for. Some people around town had already heard about him. We put our heads together and decided he was still on the bottom of Pactola Lake. Nobody but us knew any different.

And so it was done. Six hands came together as one, and Attila's paw made seven. We swore ourselves to secrecy forever. The pact sealed, we came down off the mountain.

When Quinn and I got back to the house, the message

light on the phone was blinking. It was my dad. He had called to tell us he'd been helping Uncle Jake move the household stuff from Lead to the trailer in western Wyoming. They'd emptied the house and would be coming back to Hill City tomorrow. No sign my dad had heard anything about what had been going on here.

When Quinn heard the message about emptying out the house in Lead, he dropped his head. "I can't believe this is really happening," he said, and then he went silent on me. We went outside to play some one-on-one. Quinn had a lot of frustration to take out. Just like old times, he had a step on me. He kept stopping me cold, and his shots fell with a vengeance.

Late the next morning we heard my dad's truck coming up the driveway. We went out to greet them. Quinn's eyes went to the back of the truck, all loaded with stuff. "What's that all about?" Quinn said under his breath. I was just as puzzled.

"Brought your things, son," Uncle Jake said as he jumped out of the truck.

"Huh?" Quinn replied.

"I've been thinking about this a whole lot. It's just going to be so much better for you here, and you can go to high school with Brady."

Awesome, I wanted to shout, but I held back. This was Quinn's moment, not mine. I was remembering what he'd said on the summit of the Iron Mountain Road: "You couldn't pry me out of the Black Hills with a crowbar."

Quinn wasn't answering his dad. He was looking away, at his stuff piled up in the truck, and he didn't look happy at all.

"You don't understand, son. I'm telling you, I'm okay with leaving you here. C'mon, we've talked about it."

"But we never decided."

Quinn's eyes went from the truck to our bikes leaning against my dad's shop.

Say you're good with staying, I thought. Why aren't you saying it?

Quinn kicked at a pebble on the driveway, and missed. Finally his eyes found his father's. "Here's the deal," Quinn said. "I've been thinking a lot, too."

Something you haven't told me? I wondered.

"I can live in that trailer," Quinn said. "I can go to school in Wyoming."

Uncle Jake was shaking his head. "Course you could, but that doesn't mean you should."

"*Should* is what I'm talkin' about," Quinn said forcefully.

"How's that, son?"

"We should be together, that's all."

"As much as that means to me to hear you say that, think about it. This is what you wanted, for a lot of good reasons."

"Not anymore. I just can't picture us not being together."

"I'll only be working in Wyoming for a year or two. And you better believe I'll be visiting here every chance

I get. We'll still see a lot of each other."

Just go with it, I tried to tell Quinn telepathically.

Quinn didn't hesitate. His voice was firm. "Sorry, Dad. We're sticking together. *Where* doesn't matter."

Uncle Jake's eyes were going misty on him. "You're not going to let me put my foot down, is that what you're telling me, son?"

Quinn's laugh finally broke the tension. "That's about the size of it."

My dad and I laughed, too, and so did Uncle Jake. We went inside to put some lunch together.

As soon as it was just the two of us, I made sure Quinn knew how I felt. "I get it," I told him, "and I'm really proud of you."

"Thanks, Brady. I knew you'd understand."

After we ate, Quinn and I carted his stuff over to his dad's truck, and they took off for Wyoming. Quinn got registered for school there, signed up for basketball. My mom and my little sisters came back from Iowa. The last two weeks of August slid by with me treading water, seriously missing Quinn and waiting for school to start. My family was getting used to me having almost died.

The professor was getting ready to leave soon, heading back to England with the promise we'd be seeing each other the next summer. Dr. Ripley planned on making the Black Hills and the museum his summer home for the rest of his life.

"Isn't life marvelous?" he said at last, on the sidewalk in front of the museum. "So full of surprises."

"I wish you could've won the Nobel Prize, professor."

"For a scientist," he replied, "the prize is exploring the wonders, and I've explored quite a few. No regrets."

"You and I know there's life in outer space. I never asked you how much."

"Wouldn't we both love to know the answer to that."

"Give me your educated guess, Dr. Rip."

"Well then, I shall. The universe is teeming with life."

"Thanks," I said. "That'll give me something to chew on."

I was about to get on my bike. The professor reached out and shook my hand. "Work hard in school, Brady. You might have a future in the stars."

The morning the professor and I said good-bye was Saturday of Labor Day weekend. That afternoon was when the Carvers did their big catapult demo for half the kids in two counties.

Buzz and Max looked all buff in their sleeveless T-shirts, taking turns making announcements. Crystal was there. Sort of together, we watched the Carver boys hurl their toilets, the outboard motor, the computers, and so on, even a couple fusillades from Attila's rock pile. They raked in a mint on admissions.

The very next day, three days before school was going to start, Quinn and Uncle Jake drove over from Wyoming for our annual Labor Day weekend barbecue. Uncle Jake broke some big news. He was walking away from his new job in the gas fields. They were leaving Wyoming.

I looked at Quinn, my mind racing to grasp what this was all about.

"I lost some money on the trailer deposit," Uncle Jake told us, "but you live and learn. And what we learned was that Quinn and I belong in the Black Hills. Didn't take us long to figure that out, did it, Quinn?"

Quinn chuckled, poked his dad in the arm. "Two weeks."

As Uncle Jake went on to explain, they'd already rented a place at the Creekside, the same string of cabins where Crystal and her mom lived.

There was more going on here than met the eye, and it wasn't long in coming out. It seemed that Uncle Jake and Maggie had really hit it off that last time he came through during Sturgis week. They'd been running up big phone bills ever since.

Maybe a spot would eventually open up for Uncle Jake on my dad's crew at Crazy Horse. Meanwhile Uncle Jake had the money out of their house in Lead. He could pick up handyman jobs, cut firewood, stuff like that, enough to pay the rent. And he could start enjoying the finer things of life, like designer coffee and Maggie's company.

Quinn and I started high school together, and fall went to rolling right along. We were doing some serious running after school to get ready for basketball. The aspen leaves turned gold, and no wind came to blow them off. The days grew shorter and the tourists were all but gone. Mornings were crisp, and afternoons warm and glowing under deep blue skies—a classic Black Hills Indian summer.

Uncle Jake and Crystal's mom were glowing, too. I was kidding Quinn about whether he might find himself with a stepsister one of these days. Quinn didn't laugh. He thought it was a serious possibility, so much so that he had decided against asking Crystal out.

"Tough luck," I told him, but I couldn't keep a straight face.

"You're such a fungus, Brady. Go ahead and make your move before Buzz does."

"Buzz? You gotta be kidding."

"Seriously. I just wish Crystal had seen you do your buffalo vault."

"I guess I'll have to make it on my own merits instead of Fred's."

"You miss Fred, don't you, even if he was trying to kill you?"

"In a way, sure."

"I thought so."

"You were lyin' about Crystal and Buzz, right?"

"Talk to her, Brady."

"Soon."

"Tomorrow."

"Tomorrow," I promised, and I did. I asked Crystal to the Homecoming Dance and she actually said yes.

Well, this is where I'm going to leave off, but I should

mention that I find myself watching the stars and the planets more than ever. Mars disappeared over the horizon about the middle of September, but it'll be back. As long as I live, I'll always have an extreme connection to the Red Planet.

Sometimes when I'm running after school, or during certain classes when I'm bored out of my skull, my mind goes for a bike ride down the Mickelson Trail, hangs a right at Custer, and pedals up that Forest Service road.

I hike across that mountainside through the fallen timber, and I squeeze into the Halls of the Dead. In the Palace of the Dead King, I sit on that slab where they laid me out, and then I visit the Abyss of Hades to pay my respects to Fred.

Can you hear me, Fred? Bide your time, space traveler! Who knows, in another million years, a giant asteroid might strike the Black Hills of South Dakota and you'll get blasted into space again.

Meanwhile, buddy, I'll be thinking of you. You rocked my world.